Always on My Mind

by

Andrea Downing

Always on My Mind

Cover Art by *Kim Mendoza*

The Wild Rose Press, Inc.
PO Box 708
Adams Basin, NY 14410-0708
Visit us at www.thewildrosepress.com

Publishing History
First Cactus Rose Edition, 2020
Print ISBN 978-1-5092-2968-0
Digital ISBN 978-1-5092-2969-7

Published in the United States of America

"Go back to bed, Cassie. Before something happens we'll both regret."

"How do you know I'll regret it?" She balanced herself on the edge of his bed and modestly crossed her legs. "I can't sleep," she murmured once more. "All those animals making noise."

He threw his head back and laughed so loud Cassie jumped up. Ty's words about sticking with "his own kind" floated through his mind.

"What the hell's so funny?"

"You are." He pushed himself up in the bed, unbuttoning the top of his pajamas and wriggling his arms out. "Here. Put this on, for chrissake. Cover yourself up, will ya."

She pulled the top out of his hand, a frown furrowing her face. "I didn't come in here to seduce you. I just don't like—"

"Yeah, yeah, I know—the animal sounds. Get in." He threw the cover back and shuffled over to the side of the bed to make room for her. "What did ya undress for, anyway?"

"I was hot. And that old, worn nightie you gave me was itchy."

He rested his head back on the pillow, cupped in his entwined fingers. He stared at the ceiling as Cassie tried to snuggle up to him, but he did nothing to encourage her. As she tried to rest her head on his chest, he gave up, wanting the feel of her velvet skin, the silk of her hair. "Oh, come on, then, come here." And he wrapped his left arm under her and pulled her to him.

Praise for Andrea Downing

"*DEAREST DARLING* by Andrea Downing is a page turning mail order bride tale that doesn't really follow the standard formula. Instead, the plot is fresh—after all, it isn't often that a story starts out where the wrong woman receives tickets West and decides to use them!"

~*Brenda Casto, Readers' Favorite (5 Stars)*
~*~

"*LOVELAND* is a fantastical frontier epic! The author does such an incredible job of immersing the reader in the old west that they can nearly feel the grit of the dust on their face."

~*Sandy Ponton, InD'Tale Magazine*
~*~

DANCES OF THE HEART: "What a storyteller Ms. Downing is! She knows just how to word her story to keep you interested but also engage your other emotions. The flow of this book is amazing and the characters delightful…"

~*Melanie/KissablySweet1, Have You Heard My Book Review (5 Stars)*

Dedication

For those who lived through the Seventies...
and lived on to tell the tale

Acknowledgements

My sincere thanks to Megan Smith Wachtel, Patti Sherry-Crews, and my daughter, Cristal Downing, for setting their educated eyes on the manuscript at various stages and helping it become the final story.

I am further greatly indebted to Angela Vernon, resident of Bolinas CA, for her patience with me over a lengthy correspondence regarding life in Bolinas during the Seventies. Any misrepresentations are purely the fault of the author's vivid imagination.

Last, but certainly not least, my heartfelt thanks to my editor, Nan Swanson at The Wild Rose Press. Authors have a voice and a vision, and stories in their heads, but sometimes we fall short of the techniques necessary to make the book a novel our readers actually want to finish. Nan has certainly made my story a stronger, tighter book, and for that I am sincerely grateful.

Part One: Chapter One

1972

"Sometimes the most important words are the ones that you leave unspoken."
~Mark Chesnutt, lyrics, "Almost Good-Bye"

The mirrors.

What attracted his attention at first were those little mirrors on her blouse with the embroidery around them, *they* captured his interest. They caught the light, dim as it was in the dancehall. As she moved slightly, shifted first this way, then that, the mirrors glinted, winked at him. In the smoke, she looked ethereal, not like someone of this sphere, other-worldly, as if she might disappear without a trace and he'd go on to think he had imagined her. But there she was, auburn hair pulled back at the sides and clipped to hang over her back, a heart-shaped face, and a wide smile that disappeared at the words of some fawning guy who was all over her.

Cooper Byrnes knocked back the last of his beer and almost missed the bar as he put his glass down behind him, spellbound.

He believed her eyes were blue, a rough-seas blue, dark, not that he'd ever seen the ocean himself, but those eyes brought that to mind. Her blouse hung loose over some bell-bottomed jeans that had somehow been frayed, threads hanging from the bottom then braided, tatters in the knees patched in different colors, bleached-out spots along the legs. *Why would anyone do that to a good pair of pants?* She had sandals on and, for a moment, he wondered if she could dance in those if he asked her. He leaned back on the bar as he slouched onto a stool. The jukebox was playing "King of the Road" as the screen door to the dancehall repeatedly slapped open and shut.

"Ridiculous, ain't it, them hippies? Them boys with that long hair and all." Ty Hart sauntered over and stood eyeing the aliens. "There were another bunch of 'em in here a minute ago—good riddance is what I say." His glance shifted from Coop to the girl and back again. "You haven't taken your eyes off her the whole time I've been watching. Don't tell me you like that?"

"She's not a 'that,' she's a 'she,'" he mumbled without turning to his friend. "I'm fascinated." He shifted his Stetson with one finger to alleviate some sweat under the band before he tapped it back into place once more.

"Well, she's not a bad looker, Coop, but for chrissake. She won't know nothing about living out here."

He snapped around. "I'm not marrying her, for heaven's sake." He met his friend's glare with a snarl before he pivoted back to watch the strange couple. "Just…looking."

Ty leaned on the bar as if he might fall asleep, head in hand. "Me, I like a real woman." He straightened up. "Stick with your own kind, Coop. Don't go chasing after something that'll only bring heartache in the end. Think about what you'd like to settle down with. That's my motto."

"Yeah. That's your motto until you feel like screwing around. Then your motto is to take what you can, where you can."

Ty snorted. "Might be. Might well be." He yawned. "Tell ya what. We can play our old game of who gets the gal. Come on over. Let's get rid of that loser she's with, and see who gets laid tonight."

Coop thought his gaze must be burning through the girl's blouse by now, and as if it were, she tilted her head with a glance his way before switching back to her friend. He bit his lip to stop himself from smiling. He knew it. She could feel his stare. He shook a hand at the bartender for a top-up, laid down some cash, and nodded to Ty. "All right, then. Let's see who she prefers—if either."

She certainly didn't seem to be enjoying the company of the kid she was with.

He picked up his refreshed drink, and the two men strolled over. It wasn't until he got close that he saw she had feathers attached to her hair, caught in the clip at the back of her head. He scowled.

"You an Indian?" He slugged down some beer, never taking his sight off the girl.

"Oh, jeeeeeez." The fawning boy took a step back and wrinkled his nose, his gaze running over Coop, sizing him up. "You wanna play cowboys and Indians, do you? Where's your six-shooter? Your horse?"

"Shut up, Dave. Don't be an ass."

"Yeah, *Dave*, don't be an ass." Coop smirked at the boy, took a sip of his beer, while turning his attention away from the girl a moment. He nodded toward Ty, the slightest movement, then reached past the girl and left his beer on a windowsill. "You have a problem, *Dave*?"

"Yeah, I have a problem. I have a problem with you coming over here and criticizing my girl."

Disbelief stopped him in his tracks. "You his girlfriend?"

"No, I'm not." Her voice carried a decisive note, almost disgusted at the very thought. "We were just traveling together. With some others. He's been bugging me ever since."

The band started playing, back from its break. "Wichita Lineman." The singer had a mellow voice but wasn't a good imitation of Glen Campbell.

Ty had his arms crossed against his broad chest. "Sweetheart, you look like you should have better taste than to be hanging around with this piece of crap. Come on an' dance. See what it's like with a real man."

The girl scanned Ty, then her gaze met Coop's for a brief moment before she glanced away. "I don't think so. I'm waiting for my friends to come back."

"And then what?" Coop didn't take his gaze from her. He felt a kind of current between them. "C'mon, have a dance." He extended his hand, but the girl ignored it.

The two cowboys had several inches on Dave, whose glance now shifted around, speculating. "Why don't you just get lost," he said at last.

"Why don't you?" Coop kept staring at the girl, but his remark was aimed for Dave, pitched low and slightly threatening. He swiveled suddenly toward Dave with a more meaningful stance, hands balled up on his hips, fists at the ready.

"I… Come on, Cassie, let's get outta here, away

from these hicks. We'll catch up with the others." Dave made a move to get hold of the girl.

Any response she might have made was lost as a rowdy group of several more hippies crashed in. The door whined and smacked closed once more. They almost fell upon each other as they faced the two cowboys. The laughter came to an abrupt halt as they tried to size up the situation.

"Hicks, huh?" Ty's eyes narrowed as he leaned toward Dave.

Dave, no doubt feeling somewhat more bolstered by his friends, sneered, "These two *cowboys* have been bothering Cassie and—"

"No, they haven't!" Cassie glared at Dave before switching her gaze back to Coop with an apologetic shrug. "They haven't bothered me at all."

A petite girl who had just come in with the others giggled. "Cowboys!" Glazed and slightly unsteady on her feet. "Real cowboys!"

Coop exchanged a glance with Ty before Ty's fist came to meet Dave's jaw. The petite girl screamed, and the music stopped as more of the regulars joined the fray. Coop dodged a fist, swung at one of the hippie boys, then grabbed Cassie's hand and pulled her after him out a side door into the blanket of night.

"What are you doing? Aren't you going to help your friend?" She was breathless, and he wheeled back to her, the dark now hiding her features, the warm night air of May cloaking him in damp. He clutched her hand still, small and soft in his.

"You must be joking. Ty's a national roping champion; he has more muscle than the lot of your friends combined."

"Yes, but…"

"He'll be okay. Someone will come to his rescue if he needs it. Which I doubt." He leaned against the wall of the dance hall, still holding onto her, pulling her toward him, her beauty a magnet. "So where in the hell did you come from?"

"Boston. Why?"

Coop tapped back the Stetson on his head, clutched her hand a bit tighter, absentmindedly rubbed the satin skin, his thumb making a little circle on the back, near her knuckles. "Just wondering. I thought maybe you came from another planet or something." He hadn't meant the question in the geographical sense, but more indefinite, hypothetical. It amused him she had answered with her hometown.

She laughed, a sound like the wind chimes he recalled his mama had hung outside the front door to catch the breeze and brighten her day.

"Boston," he repeated. "Well, that sure is a ways from here."

Cassie gently released her hand. "Four of us are traveling together. To California. San Francisco. Stopping to see things, and we met those others who were headed here and heard it was nice. *Jackson Hole*—it sort of conjures up the West. It—"

The sound of wood splintering, like a chair being smashed, and then a shot came from the dance hall.

Cassie flinched.

He laughed. "It is the West. What did you expect?"

Cassie gasped. "Was that a shot?"

"Blanks, most like." He was amused at her panic. "It's just to bring the fighting to an end."

"Is there often fighting here?"

6

"Only when we're called 'hicks.'" He scrubbed over his face with his hand, considering her. "So those are your friends?"

"I knew Binky in college, the little girl who wanted to meet cowboys."

"Ah."

"Ah?"

"Well she seemed…what?…happy to find 'real cowboys,' if that was Binky."

"Yes, that was Binky. Dave I didn't know before or I'd never have traveled with him. He's been a pain ever since we left Boston, but he's Binky's brother's friend. I think Steve—Binky's brother—was hoping to tie up with me and that Binky and Dave would hit it off, but it hasn't worked out like that."

Coop took in a breath and let out a slow smile. "Must be really tough to have so many men after you." When she didn't respond, he asked, "What did you expect to find in Jackson Hole?"

"I don't know." She wheeled away from him, a few steps into the dark of the trees.

She was a strange creature. Young. College educated, no doubt, and just finding her way in the world. He wondered if it was freeing to be like that, to pick yourself up one day and just head out into the world, no responsibilities, nothing to tie you down, hold you back. Then again, without an attachment to a place or land, what were you? The proverbial rolling stone.

He bit a hangnail from his thumb. It was all so foreign to his thinking. His family had lived on their land for generations, never left it, simply worked it, handed it on. There may have been times when some small piece had to be sold, or another piece bought or whatever, the original house replaced and all, but his connection to that little piece of America had remained and would remain. He had no hankering to do anything else, no yearning for the freedom of travel.

"I left my beer in there, if it hasn't been spilt. Come back in." He reached out and flicked the door back open.

The girl hesitated. "You haven't told me your name."

"Cooper Byrnes. Why?"

"*Why?* I like to know who I'm speaking to, that's why."

"Well. Now you know."

"Don't you want to know my name?"

"It's Cassie, from what that jerk said."

"Cassie Halliday."

He extended his hand as if to shake hers, but as she held hers out, he grasped it and didn't let go. Kissing her went through his mind, and he certainly was inclined that way but decided it wasn't time yet. If ever. Forget about the game with Ty, though maybe Ty was right—he should stick with his own kind, the ranching community, westerners who had roots here, settled people who knew where they belonged, didn't always ache for something more, something they couldn't have.

"Let me go get that beer, and maybe we'll have a dance," he said at last.

****

He was alien, an oddity. But then, that's why she was traveling, to see the unusual, get outside of her own little world, meet people who had different ideas, broaden her mind and learn to think in a different way,

8

see if people acted differently from those back in Boston. And then there would be Haight-Ashbury and independence and a new life. The clothes he wore were like a costume and made him even more foreign—the hat, the snapper shirt with a string tie, the pressed jeans, and boots. And then the short curly hair with sideburns. She liked his face, found him attractive—brown eyes like rich chocolate, the parenthesis around his mouth when he smiled. And the voice—a low tone, like a bass tuning up with a bit of gravel caught amongst the strings.

He didn't offer to buy her a drink, but maybe that wasn't the done thing around here. He certainly knocked back his own, wiped his mouth with the back of his hand, and stood there eyeing her as if he were trying to decide what to do next. She felt like a slab of meat he was considering eating, uneasy in his gaze. She turned to watch the dancers, thought of getting away and finding her friends, but going back to the situation with Dave seemed so much less appealing than staying with this Coop.

Someone had cleared the mess but left the leg of a broken chair leaning against the bar like a policeman's baton waiting to be used. The smoke from everyone's cigarettes irritated her eyes, and she wondered if her makeup had smudged as her eyes teared. The smell of spilt beer fought with the smoke as Elvis started singing "Always on My Mind" from the jukebox.

Cooper tapped her elbow. "You dance?"

"Not like that." She watched as couples circled about the floor in slow steps. "I could try, I suppose."

Cooper grimaced. "Come on, then." A note of reluctance colored his voice. "Let's see what you can do."

He took her hands, placed her left on his shoulder and rested his right on her back to guide her. She felt like a fool, there among the women who knew the steps, exactly how to dance, wearing their flared skirts and frilly tucked-in blouses. She stumbled, but when Coop caught her and tapped her along, she followed.

He was much older than she, and she felt slightly uncomfortable in his arms, no doubt an experienced man. The thought of sleeping with him vaguely crossed her mind, but she wondered if older men had more expectations and she wouldn't know what to do, or even want to do it.

"I like this song." It was an offering, an *I'm not as different as you might think* she was giving him.

"You like Elvis?"

"Yeah. I don't know much about him, other than what I've seen on TV. But I like him. Though I like Dylan better, of course."

Cooper snorted. "Of course. All that freedom stuff. You all back east are really big into freedom until you get called up to serve. Then you find a way out, grad school or what have you."

Was that bitterness in his voice?

"I don't see you serving your country." She glared at him, then looked away.

Coop heaved out a breath. "They won't take me. I got a II-C—agricultural deferment due to being the only man in my family working my ranch."

"So you found a way out."

"Against my will. I'll bet you anything somewhere in your family is a brother or cousin or some such who got out because he didn't *want* to fight and went off to some fancy school or whatever, happy as you please."

She knew he was waiting for a response, baiting her. "I haven't got a brother; I'm an only child. And anyway, we're certainly not rich enough for some fancy grad school, as you put it." Something suddenly struck her, and she glanced around. "Shit, where'd the others go?"

"What others? Your friends? Probably kicked out for fighting."

She took her hands away, stood staring at him, her eyes stinging as tears began to blossom. "They get kicked out, but your friend—Ty?—who threw the first punch is sitting there as if nothing happened?"

"Absolutely. He's a regular. Of course they're not going to throw him out. When will your friends come back here? Never, I'd guess. Ty comes every week. He wouldn't have caused trouble if your pal Dave hadn't started it."

She scrambled in her jeans pocket and pulled out a small plastic packet followed by a bill. "Shit," she muttered.

"You always talk like that?"

"Like what?"

"That word. I don't often hear a woman say that, not leastways a nice one."

She stuffed the five dollars and the stash back into her jeans. "You've got to be kidding. Are you living in some time warp here? Men are allowed to use some words women aren't? You must be joking!" Panic started to rise within her, the thought of being left with this guy worrying.

Coop got hold of her arm and yanked her out of the way of the dancers. "Such a pretty little thing and such an ugly word coming out of that rosebud of a mouth."

But all she could do was bite her lip to try to stop the tears. Where were her friends? She didn't know where their van was parked or where she might spend the night.

"What's the matter now? You trying to figure out how to smoke that crap you have there?"

"No, no, of course not. I just don't know where the van is. We parked on some side street and strolled around the town a while before coming here."

"What van?"

"The van we're all living in."

"Living in? *All of you, together?"*

"Four of us. What, you think we're staying in some fancy hotel?"

Cooper ran his hand over his face, his eyes still on her. "Look, you can come home with me, and—"

"Ha! You think I'm easy, that you can just take advantage because I'm from out of town."

"Oh, for chrissake. I'm not going to take advantage of you. Don't you fret. There's a spare room where you can sleep for the night, and in the morning I'll have someone, if not myself, find your friends for you. Shouldn't be too difficult. It's a small town. Or would they leave without you?"

"No, I don't think they'll do that." She couldn't read his thoughts, whether he was genuinely concerned for her or trying to get her into his bed. And she wasn't sure about where her friends might be, but then that psychedelic painted VW bus shouldn't be too hard to spot in daylight. And she didn't fear him, thought he was probably a man of his word, though she wasn't sure why.

"Well, what is it, then? You wanna sleep on the street? It's a warm May night, might only be a bit of frost later—"

"Yes, if you have a spare room."

"Right. I'll just have another beer before they shut down."

Chapter Two

She'd never been in a pickup before, though she knew her father, an electrician, had them for his company. This one smelled of wet dog, or at least wet fur or wool, and cigarette smoke, though Coop hadn't lit up.

She liked watching his arm reach out to change the gearshift, the rolled-up sleeve displaying a cast of dark hair above his wrist and strong manly hands below. She didn't feel fear, just a shade of uncertainty if she had done the right thing in going with him, though he still seemed harmless enough. Then she spotted a pack of Camels near the gearshift and guffawed.

"What're you laughing at?" Coop's mellow bass seemed to be disembodied in the darkness.

"You don't smoke Marlboros, you smoke Camels. I always think, when I see the Marlboro Man, all cowboys must smoke Marlboros."

"Yeah, well…"

The pickup jerked over a cattle guard and rumbled up an unmade road. She tried to see into the black outside, but there were only shapes, amoeba-like, indecipherable to her, blending with her own reflection. She wound down the window and let her hand feel the cool air. Somewhere a horse whinnied, and another replied with a snort. When Cooper pulled up at a house, no light was burning, and she could hardly make out its shape or size, only the reflection of the moon in a window.

He jumped down from the truck and stood, hands on hips. "If you're waiting for me to open your door for ya, you'll be there 'til hell freezes over. You all want Women's Lib or what have you, and then you won't get off your asses to pull open a door."

"I wasn't waiting for you. I'm trying to find the handle." She scrabbled around in the blackness.

"Oh, for pity's sake." He marched to her side and yanked the door open. "Come on, then."

She jumped down as dogs started yowling from inside the house.

"Shut it, Wayne! Elam!"

Cassie's face scrunched. "You name your dogs after western actors?"

He studied her for a second, lips turned up in a half smile. "You name yours for the Beatles or something?"

"I don't have a dog." She couldn't hide a shade of petulance in her voice, then felt perhaps she should act a bit more adult.

"You're not afraid, are you?"

"No, of course not."

"Well, then, follow me."

As he opened the front door, he reached around and flicked a switch on. The dogs bounded over, sniffed her, up close and personal. Coop, embarrassed by it, pulled them off her. "I'll just get them out." He sounded apologetic.

Left alone, she moved through the room they had entered, apparently the main living room, large, not what she expected, more homey and well kept than she would have thought, comforting almost. Leather couches, warm wood, framed photos everywhere, an Indian-type rug and pillows, though she found the antler chandelier and sconces atrocious. Definitely not Boston.

"Make yourself at home." His voice came from somewhere down a hall. "Can I get you anything? A beer?" He suddenly appeared where the hall met the room, barefoot, a beer in his hand, his hat off.

She could see him clearly now, a scar above his left eye marring what was actually a very pleasing face. She wished his hair were a bit longer, but otherwise she found him appealing, alluring even. Still somewhat stoned from the pot she'd smoked earlier with her friends, she felt for the nickel bag in her pocket and wondered whether he would share it with her. She perched on one of the sofas.

"Do. You. Want. A. Beer?"

"No, no, I really should go." She didn't know where that came from, but it suddenly seemed a dumb thing she had done, coming here with him, not looking for her friends, even if she did feel safe with him. His manliness compared to Dave and Steve comforted her, his maturity. But it also scared her in some way. Sex with him would be different than with one of the boys. "I should really go," she repeated.

Disbelief spread across his face. "Well, I sure as hell am not driving out again. I don't know where you think you're going this time of night."

She looked at the clock above the mantel. "It's only ten. They've probably moved on to another bar. In town."

"Okay. You gonna walk the seven miles into Jackson now?" He tipped up the bottle he was holding to his mouth, then wiped the sweat of it on his jeans, shook his head and disappeared down the hall once more, before coming back to her. "Look, I thought we'd agreed you stay here for the night. In the morning, we'll go look for that van. You can't start searching about back in Jackson now."

"No, I guess not. Do you mind if I smoke? Have you papers, by any chance?"

"I haven't got papers, no. You wanna smoke that garbage, you get your own dang papers."

"Well, I would if I could get back to Jackson."

"So, you'll have to wait 'til tomorrow. Have a beer. Join me in a beer."

"I don't like beer, quite honestly. I'm not a big drinker." She couldn't read the look this had provoked, but if she had to name it, she figured he was pensive.

Coop sighed. "I'm gonna have a sandwich. You wanna come on in the kitchen?"

She traipsed after him, his feet silent on the wood floor as her flapping sandals counted off her steps. There was a staircase to her right, its polished wood a warm honey color as if wear had pared back years from it. The kitchen looked modern, recently done, with blue-and-white metal cabinets around the wall, an electric stove, and a dinette set of matching blue plastic seating with a chrome-and-laminate table. Coop pointed for her to sit at the table, but she ignored him; instead, she rested an elbow on the white-and-blue marbled worktop and watched as he pulled things from cupboards and the fridge. He was obviously used to living alone, doing things for himself.

She liked the way he'd taken control. There was no indecisiveness the way there always was between the foursome in the van, long discussions about which route to take, where to stop, what they had money for. Suddenly, she was surprised he was not married and apparently without a girlfriend.

"You want a ham sandwich? Beef?"

"I don't eat meat."

Coop's hand stopped in midair as he turned toward her, his face reddening. "It's people like you gonna put me out of business. Dang country's falling apart as it is."

"Well, that's thanks to sending men off to die in a country we have no business being in."

He slammed the bread in his hand down on the counter. "Those men are dying to keep you safe, so them Commies don't start coming over here and getting ideas."

"That's ridiculous. You really think a bunch of Vietnamese are going to come to the United States and take over? Just fly in on Pan Am or TWA or something and overtake the government?"

"They don't have to come here. They do it bit by bit. First Viet Nam and China, and the rest of Southeast Asia, then India, then Africa, then—"

"Oh, stop." She wandered off to look at the pottery geese flying across the wall, ignoring him, as if she could escape his conservative ideas. Then she spun back.

He was still standing there, staring at her as if she had suddenly appeared and he didn't know where she had come from. Almost in slow motion, he opened a drawer, drew out a bread knife, and began to cut slices. "I have cheese if you want that." The words were just above a whisper.

"Yes, please." Coming back to him, she stood watching for a moment as he got his sandwich made, then went for her cheese. "Should I make it? Have you any lettuce? Tomato?"

Coop reached into the fridge and brought it all out, turned to her, and stopped. His chest heaved with a breath before he set the items down on the counter. "There you go." The tone of his voice had changed. It was softer, gentler somehow.

She came forward, picked up the knife, and struggled to slice the bread. Her battle elicited a snort from Coop.

He held his hand out for the knife once more, met her glance as he took it, his hand grazing hers. She suddenly wanted him to hold her, tell her it would all be all right, they'd find her friends. If that was what she wanted.

He cut the bread.

Something between them had shifted. He seemed a bit easier now, approachable.

"I don't know why I can't cut bread when I can do just about everything else in the kitchen. Guess I'm just used to my mother's Wonder loaf."

When this information didn't elicit any response, she shrugged and unwrapped the cheese, pulled leaves off the lettuce and rinsed them, along with the tomato. She felt his gaze, the watchfulness, the deliberation, wasn't surprised when he came closer.

"You sure are pretty." He reached over and tucked one of her loose hairs behind her ear, let his hand slide over her hair, the feathers swaying slightly. He gave a short laugh.

She felt the warmth from his body, and for a

moment an uneasiness at his proximity that she immediately cast aside. It was fine with her if he was going to make a play for her. She slid the top layer of bread onto her sandwich and patted it down before reaching for the knife once more. "You're not a madman, are you? An ax murderer?"

Coop stepped back and examined her. "I don't think so. Leastways not so you'd know. Why? Am I making you nervous, telling you you're pretty?"

"Sort of."

"Don't other men tell you you're pretty? That boy, for instance. Or the other one? You said they were both interested in you."

"No, they don't say things like that." She hesitated. "How old are you? You seem much older, but you don't look it."

"I don't? I'm twenty-nine, why?"

"I don't know, I just—"

"Well, Cassie Halliday, there's an awful lot you don't seem to know." Coop stood with his hands on his hips, a small smile turning up his lips. "Come on, we'll eat outside on the porch."

He settled on the steps rather than the rockers, and she sat next to him. Plates balanced on their laps, Coop's beer beside him, while she had opted for a glass of water. But she didn't eat or drink; she sat gazing up at the stars, so many, constellations fighting each other for space.

"That's one small step for a man, one giant leap for mankind," she mimicked in a gruff voice. "That's so amazing, so beautiful, I can't get my mind around it really…"

"What? That moonwalk?"

"Yes, that moonwalk. I suppose *you* think we should stay on earth, not explore, just work ourselves to death and never go anywhere."

"No, I don't. I don't think that at all. What gave you that idea?"

"You've been criticizing me and my friends all night."

"No, I haven't. Name one dang thing I criticized about you. One thing?"

"The fact I don't eat meat."

"Oh, that, well…"

"Yes, that. Not everyone has to live exactly the way you do, you know."

"Well, thank goodness for that. I like the emptiness here, the space. I can't imagine what it must be like to live in Boston or New York or San Francisco or some other great big city. I think I'd rather die."

She bit into her sandwich, reflected on his statement. "Well. I'm probably with you on that."

"Then why are you headed to San Francisco, for heaven's sake?"

Yes, why? "Because that's where everyone is going."

"Everyone? I'm not going. My neighbors aren't going. Ty isn't going. No one I know is going to San Francisco. Where in hell did you get that idea? What do your parents think about that?"

"I'm twenty-two, I can do what I want now, go where I want. Anyway, my dad just gave me two hundred dollars and said, 'Have a good time.' He didn't care."

"And your mom?"

"She does her own thing. Plays Canasta with her

friends, does some part-time work and stuff." Cassie glanced up at the house, looming in the dark. "You live here alone?"

"Yep. My mom moved in with my sister, over in Sheridan. Said I wasn't much company and would leave me to it."

"Leave you to what?" She could feel the crease between her brow and rubbed at it. *Not much company? What did that say about him if that's what his mother thought?*

"The ranch. She left me to manage the ranch is all." He swigged down some beer, set it on the step, and took a bite of his sandwich. "I never thought about nothing else but the ranch. It's been my life. Always will be."

"You don't want to travel?"

"Not a lot, no. What would I gain by it?"

"Learning about other people, for a start, different ways of thinking." *Gosh, he is set in his ways.*

"You think that would change me? For the better? Make me a better person?"

"It might broaden your mind a bit, make you more tolerant."

"I'm plenty tolerant, but I want to live the way I want to live. I don't need some government man coming in here and telling me what to do, some city folk or something. I'm doing just fine."

"Government man? Boy, you really have it bad." *Set in his ways, like an old man.*

They ate in silence for a while until Cooper got up and went in for another beer. The screen door bounced shut behind him. She stood and took a few steps away from the house, until the dogs started whining and barking from their kennel. She stepped back and stood staring up, the Milky Way above her, a white splash thrown across the velvet blackness. This was probably a fine place to live, a peaceful place to live, with so much space, and for a moment, the thought of being back in a city wasn't so tempting.

Coop came out, his beer in hand, and stood entranced, transfixed as she twirled around, hands out. She saw him there, just watching her, and felt a power over him.

Somewhere an owl hooted, and the horses in the pasture moved and snorted, their hooves plodding through damp earth.

She twirled, a dance to some tune in her head only she could hear, until she caught him still standing there, his hand with the beer stopped in midair.

"It's such a blast, all those stars. I've never seen anything like it."

"I guess not, in the city." He downed some beer and swung the bottle in his hand a few times. "I've got to head off to bed. Let me show you your room."

"You have a spare toothbrush?" She picked up the plates and hopped up the steps, facing him.

"I think I can find you one." Coop turned to the door and held it for her.

She slipped under his raised arm and stopped, then leant and pecked him on the cheek. "Thanks for taking me in."

****

Alone in the single bed with its lumpy mattress and smell of pine, Cassie had difficulty sleeping. The nightdress of his mother's he had given her lay on the floor, and she huddled down under the thin coverlet, feeling the cool of the mountain air through an open window. There were night noises—branches moaning and creaking as wind fingered them, twigs that snapped as some animal came by, and the occasional snuffle of one of the dogs in the kennel down below. Through the wall she could hear Cooper's even breathing, an occasional cough, the creak of his bed as he turned in his sleep, but the same sanctuary of peace eluded her. At last, she rose and trailed her hand along the wall until she found the door and made her way out. For a time, she stood in the doorway of Cooper's bedroom, only a vague glow of moonlight illuminating it.

Heading for the "free love" of San Francisco, she suddenly felt the burden of her virginity, so well preserved through the years of her all-women's college. Dalliance with various dates and a short-term boyfriend hadn't reached third base, and, aged twenty-two, the burden made her feel like a leper. She certainly didn't want anything to do with Dave or Steve, and Coop was so mature…

She could make out his form in the large bed, his knees pulled up, an arm flung off the side. He was wearing striped pajamas, buttons all done up on the top, or so it seemed. Buttoned up in more ways than one, yet unable to see himself any other way than what, most likely, his father had been. She moved a bit closer and reached out to run her fingers down the side of his face, feeling the stubble of his beard, the slack of his cheek, the set of his jaw, the rut of the scar.

Cooper jerked awake, insensible to what had happened. It took him a couple of minutes of gawking at her, his mouth hanging open, to realize who she was and where she was.

"Jesus H. Christ! What in tarnation are you doing?"

"I couldn't sleep."

His gaze swept over her nakedness, his whole body coming awake with small reluctance. In the moonlight, he could make out the gentle slope of her breasts, the dark areolae moving with each breath. Unwillingly, as if he had no control, he reached out and caressed one breast before Cassie pulled back.

"Jesus." He shook his head, sat up, and rested on one elbow to look at her. "Go back to bed, Cassie. Before something happens we'll both regret."

"How do you know I'll regret it?" She balanced herself on the edge of his bed and modestly crossed her legs. "I can't sleep," she murmured once more. "All those animals making noise."

He threw his head back and laughed so loud Cassie jumped up. Ty's words about sticking with "his own kind" floated through his mind.

"What the hell's so funny?"

"You are." He pushed himself up in the bed, unbuttoning the top of his pajamas and wriggling his arms out. "Here. Put this on, for chrissake. Cover yourself up, will ya."

She pulled the top out of his hand, a frown furrowing her face. "I didn't come in here to seduce you. I just don't like—"

"Yeah, yeah, I know—the animal sounds. Get in." He threw the cover back and shuffled over to the side of the bed to make room for her. "What did ya undress for, anyway?"

"I was hot. And that old, worn nightie you gave me was itchy."

He rested his head back on the pillow, cupped in

his entwined fingers. He stared at the ceiling as Cassie tried to snuggle up to him, but he did nothing to encourage her. As she tried to rest her head on his chest, he gave up, wanting the feel of her velvet skin, the silk of her hair. "Oh, come on, then, come here." And he wrapped his left arm under her and pulled her to him.

"I'm sorry."

"For what?" He tried to look down at her, but her face lay on his chest now, a fresh orangey smell coming off her hair, mixed with the smoke of the dance hall. "You are a strange one, Cassie Halliday, that much I'll say."

She wiggled around and got up on her elbow to confront him, the light from the window giving her a pale blue glow.

He'd never seen anyone so beautiful. He was helpless against the pull of that beauty, the closeness of her, the waves of her breath on his face, the spots of light in her eyes. The reactions of his body were a tidal wave rushing over him, and he reached up under the top he had given her and ran his hand down the slope of her breasts once more. This time she didn't pull away. His fingers found the proud nipples before seeking the core of her body.

Cassie flinched.

"You on the pill?"

"No." It was a reluctant admission. "My school doctor wouldn't prescribe it."

He scowled. "Cassie, are you a virgin?"

She bit her lip and pulled away a bit. Her eyelashes fluttered as if she was considering how to answer, but he knew it was only a yes or no question. "There's a first time for everything," she offered.

"Yeah, but…I haven't got a sheath."

Cassie reached into the opening in his pajama bottom and clasped him.

"Oh, Lord." He gave a low moan.

"I strongly doubt He's going to help now."

Chapter Three

Cassie found herself spread across his bed in the morning, Cooper gone, an indefinable dissatisfaction niggling her. There was a vague pain between her legs and the discomfort of stickiness coupled with an unrecognizable odor. She ruffled her hair as if something might be in it, then pulled herself from the bed and swooped to collect the pajama top from the floor as she stood. Still feeling somewhat dazed, she pulled it on, leaving it hanging open as the *clang-clang-clang* of some heavy metal sounded from outside.

For a moment, she stood in the doorway, glanced both ways, then made her way to the bathroom and cast off the top, turned the shower on to its hottest, and waited until warm water came through. She stepped into the tub to get under the shower, spied the green bottle of Prell, a cloth, and soap, and washed every inch of her as if she could wash away the memory of last night as well.

Last night. Cooper constantly asking her if she was all right, his moans, the weight of him, and the complete dissatisfaction as he pulled away at the last moment. His sweat caught between her breasts, the damp of the bed, his wet hair against her face. Was that what it was all about? Well, the deed was done. She'd probably remember him in years to come as "that guy in Wyoming" and have forgotten his name. She had no recollection of any feeling for him, any desire except that it all be over and done with. And now it was.

She stepped from the shower and grabbed a dank towel hanging there, rubbed her head, and dried the rest of her. The clanging noise had stopped, and downstairs she heard the slap of a screen followed by something being dropped. Boots? Then Coop's voice.

"Cassie, you awake yet?" His irritation was evident.

She went to the top of the stairs and stood, the towel drooping from a hand to cover her. "I'm awake. I just showered."

"You know what the hell time it is?" He gazed up at her, studied her, said nothing more for the moment.

She combed her fingers through her long wet hair and moved the strands off her face. She felt no immodesty at her nakedness, but didn't feel she was taunting Coop with it, either. She fumbled for a corner of the towel to wipe some drips as they slid down her nose. "No, what time is it?"

"It's ten o'clock, Cassie. I been up since five."

"Shit," she mumbled. "Ten o'clock?" she said in a louder voice.

"Gosh almighty, Cassie, for heaven's sake. Don't stand there like that; there are men about."

"What men?"

"My hands. The men who work for me."

"You employ people? I thought—"

"I don't care what you thought. Look, get dressed and get on down here. I was gonna take you into town to search for your friends."

"Right." She had an underlying sense of disappointment. He wanted her out. Used her and now was finished with her. Trash. Garbage. All that moaning and groaning and he was done. "I'll be down in a sec."

****

He cooked her bacon and eggs, then remembered she didn't eat meat and shoved the extra bacon onto his own plate. When he saw her standing there in the doorway, hair now plaited back into one long braid, fresh faced, barefoot, his heart battered his chest with strange sensations, a longing he couldn't quite fathom. He didn't know for what he longed, but it filled him with a strange emptiness. He felt as if he'd adopted a stray, an orphaned child, and part of him wanted back his freedom from her and yet the other part longed to have her, take possession, keep her.

"Here. Eat your breakfast and we'll go." The dinette chair screeched as he pulled it out and sat, but he started eating without waiting for her to join him. "Well?" he said at last. "You gonna eat?"

Cassie sniffed and pulled her chair out, reached for the plate he had left on the counter, and sat. "I didn't know you had other men working here."

"Dusty and Hank."

"Dusty?"

He felt her curious gaze as he forked up his meal. "Old-time cowboy. Works a place for a season, or used to, then moves on. Worked for my daddy some time back, showed up a couple of years ago now, surprised to find my daddy gone, and stayed on. Rents a place in town or something."

"You don't know?"

"I don't ask. Not my business. I don't go poking into other people's lives, don't want them poking into mine." He pulled over a newspaper on the table to make an end to the conversation.

But she pursued. "And Hank?"

He looked up. "What about him?"

"Well, I'm just curious. What's he like?"

"He's like a man who had time on his hands after retiring from his own ranch, that's what he's like. His son took over for him and Hank got a small spread, found it didn't keep him occupied, and now works for me. Old friend of my father's, if you must know." He pushed the paper away. "You gonna tell me where you think your friends are?"

"They were in a parking lot," she offered barely above a whisper. "Not near the square but somewhere on a side street. Do you know where that might be?"

"Nope, but I'm sure we'll find them. What does the van look like again?"

"A VW bus. It has psychedelic paintings on the side."

He had his fork half way to his mouth, but he stopped to stare at her. "Psychedelic paintings, huh? Well. That should be easy to spot, and town ain't big."

"Okay."

"Okay what?"

"Well, I guess we'll find it, then. Right?"

He didn't answer but shoved in another forkful of eggs and studied her. "You do want to go, don't you? You want to join them? All I've heard about is dang San Francisco."

"I guess."

"You guess what, for goodness' sake? Do you or do you not want to go with them?" He tapped the fork three beats by the side of his plate.

"Well, I thought I did. I mean, everyone's going to San Francisco. Haight-Ashbury. It's supposed to be where everything's happening. And you don't want me."

"Jeez, Cassie. I'm not the only alternative. Get a job, for goodness' sake. What was all your college education about anyway? You did go to college, didn't you?"

"Yeah, but...I went to an all-girls' college. I don't think they expected much of us beyond doing secretarial work and becoming wives."

"So find a husband. I don't care." He turned back to his paper.

"I know you don't care. I don't expect you to."

He let his fork clatter to his plate, and his gaze met hers. "Cassie, you're like...you're like..." He watched as a tear made its way down one cheek. "Oh, for gosh sake."

He met her sorry stare across the dinette, eggs congealing in the kitchen warmth. Outside was the screech of tires as a car pulled up, followed by the laughter and clatter of a group of people, sliding doors hitting the metal of the cab, shouts of "Cassie, Cassie, where are youuuuuuuu?"

He pushed back from the table at the same time as she and went to the window to look out. He swiveled to look at her, see her reaction. Then, with a gentle hand, he pushed her toward the back door.

"There you are!" Dave's voice had a note of happy surprise, which faded as he noticed Coop standing nearby. The boy stumbled as he went to her. "We had to ask that shit Ty where this guy lived and got directions here. Are you okay?"

Cassie faced Coop, her bare feet curling in the dirt in front of the ranch house as he stood on the steps and watched, arm up against a pillar, his own socked feet crossed. Part of him wanted his peace and quiet, his solitude back, but he already knew he would miss her, be sorry to see her go.

She turned back to Dave. "Of course I'm okay. I'm just—"

"Well, get your shoes or whatever and we'll go off. We should get to Salt Lake City this afternoon and stop there before heading west again."

"I…"

"She doesn't want to go with you." He heard the reluctance in her voice, came down the steps, and stood in front of Dave, challenging. "She's changed her mind."

Cassie pivoted to glance at Coop. Surprise mixed with uncertainty faded as a small smile turned up her lips. For a moment, the others were silent, standing there, stupefied. "I…" she began again. "I'm staying here." She felt bolder, more self-assured.

"You must be joking." Dave's shifty glance skimmed from one to the other. "Cassie?"

Needing reassurance, she turned to look at Coop, then turned back to Dave. "I'm fed up with traveling in that bus and I like it here. In Jackson."

"She's staying here," Coop said. "At least for now."

Perturbed at this news, the other two friends started to turn back toward the bus. Steve drew out a satchel, then scribbled something on a piece of paper before handing both to her. He nodded before he disappeared into the confines of the van.

Dave stood there gawping. "You're gonna stay *here?* With *this* guy? On a ranch? You're not coming to Frisco?"

She glanced back at Coop for confirmation.

He stayed stock still.

She turned again to Dave. "Yes, that's right. I'm staying here with Coop on his ranch. I'll follow along when I'm ready."

"How you gonna do that? You haven't any money."

"I have money. At least some left. When I'm ready I'll come. It'll be fine. Honest, Dave. I'll be along shortly. I'll hitch."

Dave's face folded into a picture of doubtfulness. "I guess it's your choice, Cassie." He eyed Coop, then turned back to her. "Just be careful, Cass. Don't fall for this jerk. He has no real interest in you."

She stood next to Coop, doubt and insecurity filling her like water flowing into a jug. The VW bus pulled out, friends waving, and she knew she was on her own.

"Now what?" Her voice was just a whisper. "Now what?"

****

He felt like he'd taken in a stray dog or a wild animal that needed some attention. She was there before him, an oddity, not someone he would usually be attracted to but was attracted to nonetheless. The weird clothes, the sandals, the feathers in her hair, the pot in her pocket, all were things of which he didn't approve. Still, the attraction was great. This woman so different, so unusual, he was enthralled by her, couldn't wait to see what would happen next. She made his life somehow more exhilarating than it had been two days before. And could he mold her? Did he want to change her? He wanted neither, but waited to see what would unfold. Suddenly, life had got exciting. She had put adventure into his existence.

He had no idea whatsoever what she thought of this sudden arrangement. She seemed to be floating through life, a ship looking for a port, or maybe a balloon let go on the wind, eventually landing as it ran out of breeze. He knew in his heart she wasn't right for him, wasn't someone who would stay long, but for whatever time she was there, he thought his life would be a little more interesting than it had been. But then he wondered if that was what he wanted.

For a week or so he let her settle in. Cassie slept in the guest room, and he left her there. He was fearful of getting her pregnant since he hadn't had time to get into town for condoms. She seemed not to mind, to enjoy the arrangement and her life here, or so he thought. He let her sleep late, didn't complain about her habits, thought she would "find her feet." Then one day as he let the screen crash shut behind him, the smell of baking stopped him in his tracks. He'd thought all morning about what he had done, letting her stay, leaving her in the house alone, but figured there was nothing much to steal, no loose cash or valuables—his mother had moved out with those. The question of what had possessed him to let her stay circled around through his mind, and he still hadn't figured that out, but the smell of baking eased him into a sense of domesticity he rather liked. As he wondered what was in the oven, he toed off his boots and headed to the kitchen for his beer. He stopped half way down the hall and listened as the sound of the vacuum hummed from above, blended with some rock music from his transistor radio. He became aware of the scent of wood polish mixed with the something sweet in the oven—burning sugar, fruit. He took the steps two at a time and leaned in the doorway of the guest room, flicked the knob of the radio to turn it down, and watched as Cassie stomped on the foot pedal of the vacuum to shut it off.

"You don't have to do that, you know. I have a housekeeper comes in once every two weeks."

"Well, once every two weeks obviously isn't enough, or she's twiddling her thumbs while she's here." She began to wind up the cord, yanked it from the socket, and wrapped the coil on the side of the machine. "Anyway, I have to do something. I'm not just going to be your…your…whore."

"No one said anything about that. We haven't even… Did I say I only wanted you for that?" He couldn't bring himself to say the word "sex." He knew she understood what was being discussed here. He waited for an answer, but she just lifted the vacuum and headed for the door. "You got something burning in the oven, I think."

"Oh, shit!" She shoved the vacuum at him as he followed, and she ran for the steps, half jumping, half falling down them in the dash to the kitchen.

He took his time putting the vacuum back in the hall closet before he followed her. He frowned as she slid a pie from the oven, set it on the top of the stove, and shook her hands from the heat that had come through the dishcloth she held.

"You burn yourself?" He came forward and took her hands.

"No." She pulled her hands back, unable to look

him in the face.

"Pie smells good. Looks fine."

"There'll probably be some sticky bits where the sugar's burnt, and the crust is a bit overdone in parts."

"Well, heck, I don't mind. Cherry?"

"Yes. I didn't think you'd care if I used them."

He cupped her chin in his hand and pulled her around to face him. "'Course I don't mind. But you don't have to—"

"I can't just sit all day."

"Okay. Suit yourself."

No doubt emboldened by his positive response, she asked, "Can we go into town one day and get some other stuff? I can cook. That's one thing I know how to do. My mother said I was born in her kitchen. I've been cooking and baking since I was little. But I haven't much money."

"You don't need money. I'll pay for food. You find what you want to do and do it—as long as you don't get in the way of the men and all. You can get really, easily hurt on a ranch if you don't know what you're doing. I don't want trouble."

"Okay."

He suddenly worried, "You got a tetanus shot? You need your tetanus shot up to date."

"I don't know."

"Well, stay away from the barns and be careful 'til you get one." He reached into the fridge and brought out a beer, rummaged in a drawer for the bottle opener, said, "And as for that other stuff, I certainly don't want you for that. Had a better time elsewhere, if the truth be told. I just thought…"

She waited but he didn't continue. Staring at the

pie, she offered, "You want me to go, just say so. It was you who spoke up and told them I was staying."

"I thought that's what you wanted, not to be with that Dave you said was bothering you. And didn't you say you wanted to learn about 'other' people, something like that, broaden your mind? So here we are. I'm 'other people' and I'm gonna broaden your mind." Amused with his own view of the situation, he took a swig from his bottle. "Maybe get you to eat beef and all."

A small smile flitted across her face before she glanced at him. "I don't think so."

"Well, if you're cooking, you sure as heck better be cooking me meat. And if I'm paying for the groceries, they're gonna include meat. Lots and lots of meat." He grunted out a laugh and headed for the door. "What time is supper? Or we just having cherry pie, then?"

Chapter Four

Cooper felt like a husband, part of a married couple, as he strolled the aisles of the supermarket with her, pulled things off shelves, discussed what brand was best, whether the cheaper one would do, which cut of meat he wanted and how much. Cassie read labels, her gaze skimming down for whatever information she deemed necessary as he stood patiently and watched her, curious. She squeezed vegetables and fruit, scrambled her fingers through displays to find ones she believed good enough, pulled back the leaves of corn, and sniffed at melons. He liked this feeling, the sense he was part of something larger than himself, belonged to someone. And she amused him, though he had no idea what she thought, how long she would stay, what her feelings were for him.

"Wow, they have collard greens. I wonder if they have grits. I could do something southern for dinner, be a southern belle."

"They have grits, but I won't eat those greens. Hate 'em, can't stand the stuff."

"Well, you don't have to eat them. You get your steak, I'll get my greens." She plopped them in the cart he was pushing. "You're gonna be very unhealthy with all that meat. Bet you're constipated as all get-out."

"Geesh. Will you watch what you say in public?" He stopped the cart and stood and stared at her, but she paid him no mind, strolled on as if she hadn't heard.

When he caught up to her, she stood holding a bag of dried beans. "You have a pressure cooker?" she asked.

"What the hell is that?"

Cassie sighed. "I guess not." She put the beans back. "That's it, then, for me. I think we have about a week of meals here."

He studied the cart. "I sure as hell hope so. This is about three times what I'd normally get. And I haven't got in my beer yet."

"You drink too much anyway. I'm surprised you can get your work done."

"I don't drink but one beer at lunch and then after the workday, in case you haven't noticed. And I think I'm entitled to drink what I want in my own home, thank you very much."

"Just saying."

"Well, don't say. Keep your opinion to yourself."

She turned away, headed to the checkout.

He stopped to load several cases of beer onto the bottom of the cart where there was space, then pushed up behind her in the line. The woman in front, who was checking out, squinted at them and nodded to him; he nodded back before he tapped his Stetson a bit lower on his head. The woman paid for her groceries and rolled her cart away. *Damn it, be all over town.*

Cassie grabbed some cigarette papers by the cash register and had started to unload the groceries when she seemed to realize there was no automatic conveyor belt. Confused for a moment, she continued to unload the cart, until he stayed her hand.

"You pack up the bags over there. I'll empty the

cart."

Her efficiency surprised him. She sorted things into different bags as they came her way, heavy items on the bottom, eggs and vegetables and fruit on top, non-grocery stuff in another bag. Her hand stopped in mid-air when she came to the packets of Durex he had thrown in. Then she shoved them in a bag.

When the checkout girl told him the bill, he sighed and glanced at Cassie. "Jeez." He paid and took hold of the filled cart to push it out to the truck. "That's about four times what I normally pay."

"I could grow vegetables, though it's a bit late to start, I guess. June. I'll have to think if anything can be grown between now and winter. When does winter blow in here?"

"Any time."

She seemed to be planning ahead, months, and that meant she expected to stay. Maybe.

"Any time?"

"It's Wyoming. The Tetons. The Rockies. We get snow any old day of the year."

"Shit. Well…" She tilted her head, mulled this over. "I could try, I guess. Plus we'd save money with a pressure cooker 'cause then I could cook dried beans in no time, instead of all those cans."

He noticed she had said, "*We*'d save money," but let it pass, smiled to himself. The fact she saw a future there didn't escape him. "Cassie, I don't know where in tarnation I'd even buy a dang pressure cooker. Probably have to go on over to Idaho, to Idaho Falls or some such. I haven't got the time for that."

"Is there a hardware shop? They might have one. Or I could drive to Idaho if you'd lend me the truck."

He stopped in his tracks. "You drive manual?"

"No, but…it can't be all that difficult."

"I don't know. I don't think I want you going on down the Teton Pass when you don't know how to drive manual. It isn't safe."

"Can we try the hardware shop, then?"

"Nope. I gotta get home to chores. Spent enough time out with you. I usually do my shopping in the evenings."

"If I could drive I could shop on my own."

But he'd enjoyed it, doing that sort of "couple" thing with her; he didn't want to be denied that pleasure. "I'll think about it," was all he said.

"Cooper Byrnes!" came a deep voice as his friend approached. He tapped the rim of his hat to Cassie and she smiled back, but Coop moved in front of her. There was a flitter of awkwardness across his friend's face. "Haven't seen you in a while, Coop. Where you been hiding yourself?"

"Aw, you know how it is, Jake. Stuff on the ranch and all. What's been happening? You sign up for rodeo this year?"

"Yeah, I'm doing saddle bronc as usual. You?"

"Nope. No, I just really haven't got the time to compete after that winter we just had."

"I was gonna give you a call—you know that gelding you wanted to sell me a way back?"

"Yep. Still have him, still for sale." He got his keys out and started swinging them. "You give me a call, we'll sort it out."

Jake took the hint and tapped his hat again in Cassie's direction.

As soon as he had turned away, she got in the cab

and jerked the door shut.

"You slam that door one more time and you'll owe me a new truck," he said as he got in. "What the heck is bothering you now?"

"You didn't introduce me. Are you embarrassed by me?"

"No, I'm not embarrassed by you. Though you sure as heck could use a decent pair of shoes. Or boots. Or something. I just don't like other people nosing into my business. This is a small town; it'll be all over Jackson by nightfall that I got a woman with me, especially now as that Mrs. O'Connell saw us at checkout. She has a mouthpiece on her, I can tell you." He turned the key and started the motor. There was silence in reply as he pulled out onto the highway and headed for home. Her reticence prodded him, a pain. He suddenly made a U-turn.

"What are you doing now?" A note of alarm toned her voice.

"Going for your goddamn pressure cooker, that's what. What else?"

****

Cassie admired the way the men hanging around outside the hardware shop all greeted Coop, stopped him in conversation. And she laughed to herself at the way they all struck the same pose, hand on hip, boot heel resting on a step or drawing a line in the dirt, cowboy hats slouched forward, dusty jeans and even dustier boots. She knew she embarrassed Coop with her beads and her bellbottoms, so after she'd waited a minute—in which he'd ignored her completely—she strolled into the hardware shop and let the door bang shut behind her. She was beginning to realize he could be a pain in the ass, but he was her pain in the ass. At least for now.

She didn't know what half the things were but ambled through the aisles, picked up this and that and inspected them, tried to guess what some of the stuff was, what it did or what it was for. And then she spotted the seeds. A revolving rack, some of its spaces empty, others with a few packets left. Carrots, beans, peas—beets she didn't like, so left them there—leeks, winter squash. Spinach might grow…

"What are you doing? I thought we were here for a pressure cooker." Coop's hand was gentle on her shoulder.

"Yes, but…I'd like to try to grow a few things."

"And just where do you intend on doing that, Cassie? In the barn or the house?" His sarcasm hurt her when she was trying to make herself useful.

"Well, I thought…I thought there might be room. Outside. Just a small plot."

"The growing season's not long enough, and—"

"Then why do they sell seeds? If no one can grow anything, what would be the point of them selling seeds?" Her hand was on her hip, and her head tilted at him.

Coop's gaze avoided her a long minute.

"Fine." There was a huff in her voice as she started to put the packets back.

Coop grabbed them out of her hand. "Go find the dang pressure cooker and let's get the hell out of here, will ya? I've been away from work long enough. I'm not one to leave my men to do it all while I lollygag with you."

"Well, it was your idea; I never asked." She headed

off to the area where kitchen items were stacked and found the cooker.

A man behind the counter was serving someone else, so they stood aside, while yet a third man stood off at a distance. A middle-aged black man, in worn dungarees with a pleasant smile on his face, he clasped a list in one hand, his gaze avoiding Cooper as he patiently waited. She cradled the pressure cooker. Coop tapped his boot irritably, the seed packets hanging from his hand. As the first customer picked up his goods and headed away, the man behind the counter glanced first at the black man who had waited, then Coop.

"Well, Mr. Byrnes, what can I do for you today?"

He moved up to the counter but Cassie leaned the cooker on the edge and said, "Coop, that man was before us."

He turned his head to take in the black man who had been waiting. The man smiled and nodded at him but didn't move.

"Mr. Tennison don't mind waiting another bit," the hardware man said. He went to take the pressure cooker to the cash register, but Coop put his hand out.

"That's all right." His voice was quiet, sure. "I can wait, too, John, if Mr. Tennison was first."

****

The dry air of the early June heat blew in the window. She watched the passing scenery go by, her fingers arched back as if catching the breeze. She saw Cooper now in a different way, complex, maybe as uncertain of things as she was at times. During the day, he showed her little affection, concentrated on getting his ranch chores done, but at night, on their own, he seemed to be totally interested in her, almost loving despite the fact they still hadn't had sex again. Was it the drink that made him loving or the drink that prevented sex? Was he trying to slowly win her?

Her thoughts played over what had happened at the counter, whether he had done it for her or because he believed it right, that the other man should be served first, whatever color he might be. She stole a glance at his profile, lost in his own thoughts, strange man.

"Why did that man do that, do you think?" she asked at last.

He pivoted to her sharply before his gaze went back to the road. "Do what, for chrissake? What man?"

"The man at the counter. Why would he serve you first before the other man?"

Cooper frowned. "How the hell should I know? Dumb bastard. Some folks are just like that. Want a feeling of superiority so treat others like trash."

Surprised he hadn't avoided the subject, pleased at his stance, she faced her smile to the window before she turned back as he continued.

"Same as down south. Dumb bastards thinking their whole world is gonna change just because they take some Negroes into school with them. Who can figure that?"

"They don't want to be called Negroes any more. They're blacks."

"Shit." He drove for a bit before he continued. "They think changing their name or race or whatever is gonna help the situation?"

"Well. Maybe *Negro* is too close to that *other* word…you know. That's so demeaning. People don't call us Caucasians, they call us white."

Cooper seemed to ponder this for a bit, his lips

turned slightly in a stifled smile. "I don't know. Anyways, there's not a lot of them out here, so maybe folks just feel they can treat the ones that are here any ol' way. I have no idea what gets into the heads of other folks."

"Well. Thanks."

Confused, he grimaced at her. "Thanks for what, for Pete's sake?"

"For letting him go first. That was kind. It showed the man at the counter he was wrong."

"Well, heck, Cassie, I didn't do it to either please you or to teach that guy a lesson. I did it 'cause it was right, the right thing to do. Tennison was first, and even if I was in more of a rush than he seemed to be, and he didn't seem to mind, it was just right."

"Okay. But thanks anyway."

They pulled into the yard out front of the house. Coop jumped out of the cab and went round to let the tailgate down. The dogs came up, wagged their tails, and barked around him.

"I'll deal with the groceries," she offered. "You go back to work."

He didn't need to be told twice. "Don't try and move that truck now, you hear? Just leave the keys where they are."

She bounded up the steps, a shopping bag in each arm, and groped to pull the screen door open. Contentment washed over her. Inside she was greeted by the hum of the vacuum coming from upstairs. She dropped the bags on the kitchen worktop and started to go to get two more when she heard the vacuum groan to a stop. An elderly woman appeared at the top of the stairs. Gray hair pulled back framed a stern demeanor set on a face like an Indian totem, beaked nose and dark eyes: the woman glared down at her.

"Hello." Cassie tried to smile up, but the warmth wasn't returned.

"You the girl, then?"

Unsure how to reply, she just stood and stared back up into the dim light that framed the housekeeper. "I guess."

"Humph. You know everyone in town is talking. You're giving Cooper a bad name."

Her hands found her hips as she glared back. "I guess if Coop is concerned about his name he'll let me know and ask me to go, if he wants." She thought for a second. "You can see I'm sleeping in the guest room. Why don't you tell the town that?" And she marched out for the rest of the groceries.

****

At night, as Coop shuffled out of his shirt and tugged off his socks, he could make out the even sounds from the guest room, Cassie brushing her hair, like a steady heart beat, a constant rhythm, and he wished he could be the one brushing it for her. He went and stood in the doorway to her room, studied her for a second before she noticed him.

"Can I do that for you?"

She held the brush out to him, her face a picture of uncertainty and nervousness, as if he might strike her with it.

But he was gentle from the first stroke, placed one hand lightly on her shoulder to just hold the tips of her hair as he moved the brush down from the top of her head in slow, even lengths. And then he reached and moved her hair aside and arched down to kiss her neck.

He sensed her stiffen for a moment before she relaxed back into his arms as he nestled into her, inhaled the sweet scent of her skin.

"You think you could move back in with me? You know, permanent-like?"

She was still under his hand, unmoving. "Yes, but…your housekeeper said—"

"Oh, never mind what old Mrs. Craven said. It don't matter none."

"She said it was all over town, that I'm embarrassing you. And you know that's true. You never introduce me to anyone. You *are* embarrassed."

Coop collapsed down on the bed behind her, the brush still in his hand as he played with the bristles and rubbed them first this way, then that. "It's not that I'm embarrassed, Cassie. Well, maybe I am. You in those dang bellbottoms with feathers and beads. People 'round here can't fathom that, and I don't want to throw it in their faces. Anyways, it's none of their dang business who I'm with or what girl I have here."

She swiveled to face him. "That's the thing, Coop. That's who I am. And I don't know why you want me here if you feel that way. It's a mystery."

He got up, dropped the brush on the bed. "Then why in tarnation did you stay?"

"Because…because it seemed right somehow, at the time. Because of what you said. You told them I was staying, so I assumed you wanted me to."

"And I did. Still do. I just don't like other folks telling me—"

"Yeah, yeah, telling you how to live."

He blew out a breath, then grabbed her up to him with such force she was like a doll in his arms. He pressed her against the wall, his hands cupped at the back of her head as he kissed her. The firmness of his mouth was hard against her own before his tongue entered the cavern of her mouth and she at last relaxed, returned the kiss, rubbed her cheek into his hand, and her head fell back as she came up for air. She gasped, stared at him.

"Sorry," he whispered. His chest heaved with gaining breath. "I didn't mean to hurt you. Did I hurt you?"

There was a slight shake of her head. "No."

"I know it wasn't good the first time—"

"You said you didn't like it."

"I didn't mean it that way. I meant…I meant, the first time. It's never any good. You're nervous and don't know what to do, and I had to…you know. We didn't have protection. Maybe you could see a doctor and go on that pill, but I have Durex now. It'll be better. Maybe you'll relax more as you get used to it."

Beneath his hand, as he trailed fingers down from her neck to her breast, he could feel her body quiver, making its own decision for her.

Chapter Five

"Wayne! Elam!" Cassie tried to get hold of the dogs, but they were circling around and avoiding her while trampling some of her seedlings. She had managed to convince Cooper to rope off some land next to the house on the south side where it got less wind. By late June, she had planted rows, mulched and watered, and when the shoots started up in early July, squirted boiled tobacco juice from the butts of his Camels—and maybe a stolen cigarette or two—to keep the bugs off and slugs and snails away. Coop had said he'd rarely seen a slug or snail, but somehow they had appeared, a feast for them suddenly available. Now here were the dogs, trampling and laying waste to some of her hard work.

It was difficult for her to know exactly what he made of her; he rarely let on to his feelings except at night, when his tenderness surprised her. They seemed to have reached some sort of arrangement, a relationship without strings attached.

She knew in Coop's eyes she had a lot of growing up to do; in her eyes, he was staid but steadfast, settled, safe. But not to be crossed.

She started giggling uncontrollably as she went around in circles after the dogs, grabbed at their hind quarters to pull them out of the bed, one heading back in as she reached for the other. At long last, she ended up on her backside, a quaking mass of laughter that turned into sobs. She was sitting in the dirt like that when Coop rode up.

He dismounted and tied his horse to the post at the house before he strolled over. "Come here, Elam! Wayne!"

The dogs scurried over to him, tails wagging, but he kicked them away toward the house. "What the heck is wrong with you? What are you doing?"

Tear-stained and dirt-streaked, she peeked up at him. Her emotions heightened by the drugs she was on, she could look at him all day, the lean muscular frame, the Stetson slouched down, the brass-buckled belt riding on slim hips where his hands now rested. Her head tilted onto her shoulder in a wave of dreaminess.

"Shit, are you stoned?" He bent to look at her, holding her face in his gloved hands so he could peer into her eyes. He shoved her away in disgust. "Damn it, Cassie, what if one of the men saw you like this? Aren't you shamed for yourself, using that stuff? Your eyes are black as coals; it's like there're two holes where the pupils should be. Where you getting this shit from?"

"I had some left so thought I'd finish it up." She sniffed.

"All at once?"

"Huh?" She shuffled a hand in her hair and tried to get to a standing position, but only managed as far as her knees. "There was only enough for one joint. When you went over to your mother's that time, I smoked a bit."

"A bit. A bit, huh? You had a bag of that garbage, far as I remember. I don't like you smoking that crap, and I sure as hell don't like you smoking it here—

behind my back. You go round a ranch stoned like that, accidents happen."

"It wasn't behind your back, Coop. What difference does it make anyway?" She waddled to her feet. "I knew you wouldn't like it, so I smoked when you were gone, that last weekend in June. If you didn't know, what harm did it do? You drink all the time."

"I've told you before…" His gloved finger came in her face. "I can drink when I want, do what I want in my own goddamn home. And don't you forget it." He turned back to his horse, loosened the lead rope knotted on the hitching post, and started to lead his gelding away.

"I hate you!" The words tumbled out of her mouth, a frown puckering her face, contorting it. Somewhere in the fog of her mind, she knew she had to love him first before she could hate him. And she knew she didn't mean it, that love was what she felt. And it was more than his masculinity, more than his virile looks—it was the way he cared for her, even if it was often in this peculiar gruff manner.

Cooper came up, the horse's lead still in his hand, but his voice was vile, his face right up to hers. "You are free to leave any old time you want, miss. Don't you forget it. And *I* am free to send you packing if and when *I* want." He stood back and, stone-faced, stared at her to make sure she had taken that in.

She sniffed, tripped over one of the dogs, which whined pitifully, and belted into the house, the screen door bouncing back as it hit the frame.

****

Early evening, he found her curled up, her hair straggly, the dirt marks still on her face. Cooper sighed and leaned on the doorframe, considering. One moment she could be a woman, a housewife, someone he wanted to come home to; the next she was just a spoiled child. He couldn't figure it out, didn't know how to treat her, yet found he continued to want her around, didn't want to lose her. Maybe that's just the way things were and would always be with her—woman one moment, child the next. Yet he found that exciting in some measure, and appreciated the things she did around the house, the way she had made a life for herself here, had become a homemaker and lover all at once.

"I asked the men to stay tomorrow night. We play poker on occasion, and I feed them a meal so they don't have to head home and come back. You think you might rustle up something for us all? Please?" He straightened up. "I keep telling them what a terrific cook you are—when you don't try to feed me those dang nut burgers or whatever—I thought maybe you could cook something they'd wanna eat."

There was a sniff from the bed.

"Cassie?"

Another sniff was the reply.

"Look," he said coming over, "I'm sorry, but getting stoned isn't the way to deal with life."

She unfurled and faced him, her dirty, tearstained face contorted in dismay. "Neither is drinking!"

He sighed. "Look. I'm not gonna go over this with you again. I've told you before: I'm not gonna be told what to do in my own home. And I don't drink 'til after work, and I have a right to drink any old time I feel like it. But you doin' them drugs, that's against the law—"

"Well, the law is an ass."

"May be. Maybe. But it is what it is, as it stands. And I don't like finding you half out of your mind in the dirt there. What if it hadn't been me who found you? What if it was one of the men? What then?"

Cassie pulled herself to sitting and pierced him with a look. "Yes, Coop, what then? What the hell do you think would have happened? Huh? What?"

"Well, for one, I woulda been embarrassed as all get-out. It's already the talk around these parts I got a woman living with me, unwed. So if someone finds her stoned and lying in the dirt? What then?" He took a few more steps toward the bed and finally perched on the side. "I gotta live here, Cassie. Whatever you decide to do, wherever you eventually go, I'm staying here. I got roots here, and I gotta think about my family's name." He waited a moment, watching her chest heave and some tears meander down her cheeks, lost as she was. "So what are you gonna do? Cook up a storm and make me proud, show 'em *why* I got you here, or lie there like a drunken wretch—a stoned wretch, rather."

For a moment, Cassie didn't move. She reached for a tissue on the bedside table and blew into it, her eyes searching his before she made a decision.

"Well? You gonna go on down and cook up something tomorrow? Or am I gonna have to tell them we only got chips and stuff?"

One last sniff. "I'll see what we have, what I can do."

****

She hadn't been banished, nor had Coop said anything to her, but Cassie understood she wasn't wanted in the kitchen that night, that it was a men's night. Quite happy with her lot, she settled on a stair to listen for a while, the sounds of the men's voices more like grunts to each other, a foreign language she didn't understand. Yet she knew she loved that, loved them all, their ways, so different from Boston. Like hard-shelled candies with soft centers, that was the way they were. Or that was Cooper, at least. She realized that now.

"See you."

"Two pair."

"Pass me that mush she made up."

"You got more of them corn chips?"

A few syllables here, a few words there, passing for sentences—communication of a nature unknown to her. Smoke drifted out into the hall, and she figured it was probably hellish in the kitchen where they sat; the thought of the smoke with the food disgusted her. Occasionally the sound of shuffling cards would come, and she knew they were starting another game. She tiptoed to glance at the mantel clock but it had stopped.

Suddenly, the sound of a chair scraping back on the lino floor came with a voice she thought she now recognized as Ty's, from their few brief encounters.

"Deal me out this hand, I gotta piss."

She scurried to go up the steps out of sight, but Ty was already out the door.

"Well, what have we here? Little Miss Airy Fairy with her feathers and beads."

She tried to smile and remain nonchalant, but there was something about Ty she never liked, that made her nervous. Even on the phone, when she picked up, he seemed insinuating, rude. She lowered herself back onto a higher step.

"You sure cook up some strange stuff. What's that

mush you feeding us, that white stuff? It got Spanish Fly in it or something?"

"White bean paste. You don't like it, don't eat it."

"Oh, but I'm trying to figure out exactly what it is Coop sees in you, why he keeps you here. You one of them sex slaves, then? You must be pretty dang good in the sack for him to keep you on. You do him on a regular basis or something?"

"You're disgusting." She reached for the banister and started to rise, but Ty grabbed her hand. "Let go of me!"

"You know what? I think the men would like to get to see you, thank you for that fine food you laid out there for us all." He yanked her down the steps, dragging her into the kitchen behind him. "Look here, everyone. Look who I found waiting patiently on the steps to take her bow for all this food."

She struggled against his hold, but he whipped her around to the front of him and held her tight.

Coop looked from one to the other. "What are you doin', Ty? Leave her be." He stood from his chair.

"Well, I thought you'd want to show her off, Coop. All these fixings of hers you gave us, surely you'd want to bring her in for a bow. And she was just sitting there on the steps—"

"Ty, you're drunk," started an older man sitting next to Coop, "and you're probably hurting the poor thing. Let her go, take a piss, and come on back to the dang game."

A third man just rocked in his chair, watching it all unfold, quiet, his eyes shifting from one speaker to the next.

"Well, I thought you all would want to see Coop's

latest, now that he's dropped Marianne. Seems one's as good as another."

Coop scraped back from the table and heaved a sigh. "Ty, what happened between me and your sister is…between me and your sister. And she broke up with me. You can ask her. So now let Cassie go and let's get on back to the game." He reached out to release her, but she managed to pull free and started for the door.

The man who had been silent put his hand out and touched her arm.

"Ma'am, just want you to know that was a real delicious and different meal you set out for us, and it's much appreciated."

She nodded to him, glanced back to Coop, and dashed for the door and up the steps. Behind her, she could hear him say, "You know, Ty, you're a real dumb bastard sometimes. What was that all about?"

But she locked the guestroom door behind her and listened as someone, probably Ty, went to the downstairs bathroom before heading back into the kitchen and the poker game. She reopened the door to go wash and locked it again on her return. As she drifted in and out of sleep, she thought of Coop with this other woman, what Marianne must be like, Ty's sister, from a ranching family, known around town, a suitable match for him. Did the woman look like Ty? Was she tall like him? Did Coop still love her? He'd said Marianne had been the one to break up with him. Was Cassie just someone he'd picked up on the rebound to keep him company? To make Marianne think he didn't care? She couldn't get her thoughts straight.

Sometime later, she heard the low voices in the

hallway, then the consecutive start of their pickups before they drove away, followed by the sound of Coop heading into the kitchen. He must've been tidying up some before she heard his slow ascent of the stairs and halt at his open bedroom door. She raised up on one elbow to listen if he would try her door, but there was soon the sound of his boots hitting the floor in his room and his tread as he went to the bathroom.

She lay back down and fell asleep.

When she went down in the morning, the kitchen had been cleared, the dishes washed and left to dry in the rack, leftover food put away. It couldn't have been Mrs. Craven who had done this; it wasn't her day to come in.

Cooper.

What now? Was he trying to prove he could handle things without her? Getting ready to tell her to go? She started to put the remaining dishes away. The coffeemaker still offered a cup or two, which she poured into a mug. The only thing he'd left dirty was the ashtray in the middle of the kitchen table, filled to overflowing with cigarette butts. Her bug spray. He'd left it for her bug spray. It was the sort of thoughtful act she loved about him.

The reluctant groan of Coop's pickup sounded outside, followed by the squeal of tires as he pulled away. He hadn't said anything about going anywhere today, so now it all started to come together in her mind. Guilt was what had prompted him to clean up, and now he was going to see this Marianne before telling Cassie to push off. This thought grew in her mind throughout the morning as she sat with her coffee, mixed yoghurt with her homemade granola, stared out the window. While she fought this growing paranoia, she heard again Ty's words. He had reminded Coop about Marianne, and Coop now wanted to see if Ty's sister would take him back. That was it. She began to wonder if she should leave before he told her to go, pack up, hitch out.

She rinsed her dishes and headed outside to inspect the vegetable garden, pick a few things that were ready, thin out some of the growth. She tried not to think about Coop and Marianne, but then it struck her that maybe there were photos somewhere. Inside, in the living room, where they rarely sat, with its leather couches and antler chandelier, the photos stood waiting. She picked them up one by one, looked for some sign of a girlfriend. There were some rodeo shots—Coop in midair having been flung off a horse, or proudly holding up a trophy. Photos of an older couple she presumed were his parents, the woman reappearing in other pictures with Cooper, smiling. And then a young woman standing beside Coop. Was that Marianne? Coop was beaming broadly, but the girl looked more amused than anything else.

No answers here. Could be Coop's sister, now living in Sheridan.

It was coming up to noon already. Best to get his dinner going.

Back in the kitchen, she cleaned some potatoes and green beans, heated up the broiler for his steak. She heard the truck pull back up and groan to a stop. It sounded as if it was right in her garden, but she doubted he'd be that cruel, after cleaning up this morning. The clang as the tailgate came down was followed by the clatter of what sounded like wood, the shouts of men as they heaved stuff off the pickup. Curious, she pulled back the little café curtain to peep out. The quiet man from last night stood with Coop by a pile of what looked like wood panels. She dropped the potatoes and rinsed her hands before heading for the back door.

The two men turned as one to look at her. Coop had what passed for a smile on his face as she looked from the men to the pile.

"What's that?" She stepped down from the kitchen and let the screen slam shut.

"What does it look like?" Coop appeared proud of himself, as if he'd had a stroke of genius.

"Huh? It looks like a pile of some sort of wood panels."

"And what do you think we're gonna do with those panels, then?" He placed his hands on his hips as if she should know the answer immediately.

The other man just gazed down at his boots with a smile.

"I have no idea. Is this a guessing game?" She couldn't keep the hint of annoyance out of her voice.

"It's a wind break. Give your garden some protection and all."

She knelt to inspect the panels as if she would know what to do with them next. "Really?" She widened her eyes at him, trying not to smile too broadly.

"Really. Hank here is gonna help me get it up. Might be this afternoon. Got a gate and all, keep the dogs or other wildlife out."

They stared at each other for several moments. Hank glanced from one to the other, then drew a line in the dirt with his boot.

That night, she moved back into Cooper's bedroom.

Chapter Six

Coop came to understand Cassie had made an uneasy peace with Mrs. Craven, giving her excess vegetables to take home and the occasional baked pie when she could do two. He just shook his head in wonder and let it be. Cassie had been berry picking despite warnings about bears, so it didn't cost him anything, and he privately thought it a fine idea to be on Mrs. Craven's good side. He noticed Cassie mussed the guest bed when the woman was due to come, and he said nothing, supposing that, too, helped the old lady's opinion of what was going on.

By August, he realized he was controlling his feelings, holding on tight to them for fear of Cassie's leaving. He wanted her to stay, envisaged her as permanent, yet couldn't voice his emotions. Busy with chores for the coming autumn—checking stock tanks and bedding for the animals, preparing storm shelters for them, and winterizing the equipment—he decided she really ought to learn to ride, and so he showed her. He took his time to teach her, stayed patient with her mistakes, chose the calmest gelding he had as her horse, with a saddle that was on the small side for the men. Since she loved the horses and animals in general, Cassie took to riding and smiled like a loon as she attentively listened, hanging on his every word.

"Get those heels down, Cass. If you don't keep

your heels down, you'll fall off first time you ride out. You want to fall on your head or break something?" *Lord forbid.*

"I thought my heels *were* down. How far down do they have to be?"

"Down, for heaven's sake. Lower than your toes. Sit back in the saddle, it'll be easier, and move with Rowdy, with the horse."

"Rowdy?"

"Yes, Rowdy."

"As in Yates? *Rawhide*?" She held the reins loose in her hand and studied him. "You're not very imaginative."

He knew what she was thinking—first the dogs had been named for cowboy actors, and now the horse was named for a TV character. He came up to where the horse stood and peered up at her. "I don't have to be imaginative. I just need to name the horses. Doesn't make a blind bit of difference what the dang horse's name is as long as he knows who I'm calling, or speaking to." He grasped her foot. "Get that heel down, or you'll never be leaving the corral. And sit deep into the saddle so's you can move with the horse." He strolled back toward his spot on the edge.

"Okay, pard." She pressed her lips together, obviously suppressing a laugh, as he spun round.

"You think this is a joke?"

"Not at all. It's great."

"Ha!"

"No, really, Coop. I really want to learn, and I appreciate you taking the time to teach me."

"So you should." He bit his lip. "Well, I don't suppose you had much chance, growing up in Boston as you did, did you?"

"I went for a pony ride once."

He studied her for a moment, and tried to think what a pony ride might entail. "Where did that go?"

"Around in a circle. Sort of like this, only smaller, and the man led the horse around."

He shook his head. "Well, a whole lot of good that must've done."

She stared at him, wide-eyed, and grimaced. "Well, it's not like here. We don't ride much, and those that do, ride English, I guess." There was a hint of regret in her voice. "Can we go someplace yet? Ride out?"

He leaned back against the corral post and stared out beyond the fencing, out to the cows, the pastures, the mountains. He could see Dusty waving his hat around to get some calves to move. He took this all for granted, knew he took it for granted, this life, and yet he loved it without thinking about it, what it meant to him. His connection to the land. What could it be like to be brought up in a city? Or a suburb. And did she understand what this all meant to him?

"Come on, then." He sighed. "You go round a few times and try to get those heels down. I'll saddle up."

****

She never got over the fresh air out here, the sense of breathing, of taking something clean and renewing into your body. The freedom. Although there wasn't so much freedom with Coop telling her what to do at times, but it was more liberty than she had known. College, then home, then college, back and forth between the one with its schedule, the other with its comments and dictates.

"You dreamin' or something?" Coop looked across

at her as they entered the first pasture. "Keep your mind on this. Cows can be unpredictable."

"Not as unpredictable as you."

He reined in beside her. "Well, what the heck is that supposed to mean?"

Her lips turned up, but she didn't answer, didn't look at him. Finally, she just whispered, "Nothing. It means nothing."

Annoyed, he grumped, "Well, what did you say it for?"

She heard him take in a deep breath.

"You wanna try loping, then? You think you're ready?"

She could feel her face stretch into a smile as she nodded.

Coop smiled back. "Heels down, sit well into the saddle, move with the horse."

"Yes, sir!"

Later she would think she could do that every day of her life.

****

Learning to drive manual was less successful. Coop wasn't even sure why he was teaching her except that she had asked, and he considered it, thought she ought to learn in case of an emergency or some such, though what emergency he didn't know. When would he ever send her out for something? He knew he faced a series of jerks, stops, and starts that would almost make him sick, try his patience bitterly, until at last she'd get the hang of it. Yet even if she learned, he would rarely let her do the shopping on her own, would say instead he had to come along to keep an eye on things lest she buy too much, buy the wrong beer, spend too much.

Plus, she seemed to appreciate him taking her, coming with her to shop, and appreciate his company as much as he enjoyed going along.

Still, he went on with the lessons, though it tried him.

"Look, you see there are three pedals now, not two like you're used to in an automatic. That third one has to be operated with your left foot."

"Left foot, got it."

"You smile as if I'm telling you all this for nothing, but you're gonna have to be more coordinated than with a dang automatic."

"I know."

He peered at her, trying to read her mind. "It's the clutch."

"Clutch," she repeated.

He took a deep breath. "The clutch is what you need for shifting gears. See the different numbers, and the R for reverse—"

"We have R for reverse on automatic."

"Forget about automatic now, just concentrate on this, will ya?" He waited a second before continuing. "So you press down the clutch and move the stick shift through the gears to go faster. One is good for hills and steep inclines, or when you want particular control like on a very bendy road—like Teton Pass. Not that I'm ever gonna let you drive that, but it's that sort of thing."

Cassie shrugged. "I've been driving since I was seventeen. Why won't you let me drive on Teton Pass?"

He sat back, exasperated. "Well, where you gonna go down the Teton Pass, Cass? It leads to Idaho."

"I don't know. California maybe."

He could see she was trying to wind him up. He

gave her a hard stare. "Well, you leave for California in this rig, and I'll have the sheriff after you." He let that sink in, his ire mounting, but his anxiety as well. He didn't like the thought of her leaving, yet trying to say that, to find words to express that, wasn't in his nature. "You gonna learn this?" he said at last.

"Sure. Clutch to change gears, move through the numbers, R for reverse. Got it."

"Hang on, I'm not finished yet. You want to push the clutch down, release the parking brake—that thing there—turn the key and ease her into first gear."

Cassie followed his instructions, but the pickup stalled.

"Oh, for goodness' sake. Look. That there is your tachometer. It's got to get up to between 1,500 and 2,000 so's you don't stall."

"Right." She tried again, this time with a jerk.

"You're gonna ruin my gear box if you keep this up."

Cassie looked over at him, tried again, and finally got it going.

"Don't stall, don't stall! Give her a bit more gas now and move into second." He leaned back as the truck jerked its way down the ranch road. Somewhere in the back of his mind he was yelling, "Don't go, don't go," but those words would never come out.

****

He sensed they'd at last become less of a curiosity to the town, that the gossip-mongers had moved on to pastures new, and he relaxed in that knowledge. One night he decided they should go back out to where they met, show off their dancing, have a night out she might enjoy.

As she came down the stairs, he stopped in his tracks, looked up at her, thought he had never seen anyone so lovely. There she was in an ordinary pair of jeans and a checked shirt, dangly earrings the only ornament she bore.

She twirled on a step above him. "You like it?"

"Where in tarnation…when did you get those jeans?"

"Mrs. Craven took in my old jeans for me and stitched up the tears—no bellbottoms! But they do still have the patchwork pockets at the back." She turned to let him see what might be a giveaway. "I had the earrings. Do you like them?"

"Sure. Yeah." He hesitated. "And the shirt?"

"You don't recognize it?"

"Shoot. Is that the one I was throwing out?"

"Sure is, buster. I retrieved it—the tear was only slight and not where it would be in my size. Mrs. Craven cut it down for me, too." She hesitated. "I know it's not quite what the other women wear, skirts and all, but I think it'll do. Don't you?"

"Well, heck, I…I'm sure it'll be fine, Cass. I must be the luckiest man in all of Teton County."

She skipped down the steps and stood in front of him grinning.

His gaze ran over her one last time. Then he did something he'd never done outside the bedroom—he gathered her to him, cupped her head in his hands, and kissed her hard, long and deep, grasped her tightly to him because he suddenly wanted her so much. "Jeez. I better stop that," he said as he released her with care. "We're gonna end up back upstairs with no night out, if I continue that."

"I don't mind."

"Yeah, well. A promise is a promise, and I said we'd have a night out, so let's get on out."

In the truck, he grabbed glances at her as she watched the scenery go by, wondered what she was thinking. She'd seized one of his old denim jackets, which swamped her but somehow suited her and made her look like she belonged out here. And he worried whether she had a heavy coat or jacket, or maybe he should get her one before the cold weather really set in…and whether she'd stay long enough to need it.

When they entered the hall, the dancing was already under way, the band at the front in a dim orange light, while the lights on the dance floor remained bright. Coop looked around for anyone he knew, saw some friends at the bar, and guided Cassie over. "Let's join Ben and Sheila," he mumbled.

She stopped.

"What's wrong?"

"Are you sure you want me to meet your friends? I thought…"

"Come on. You look fine. What do you want to drink?"

"Um, wine?"

"Not sure how good it is here. You really ought to learn to drink beer."

He tapped his friend on the back. "What're you guys drinking? I'll get a round."

****

Two rounds later, Cassie stood uneasily, listening to the conversation between the two men—cattle prices, vet's fees, the cost of feed. The woman, Sheila, had turned toward another girl at the bar so that now she felt left out, the odd one.

Coop suddenly turned to her. "I guess we better dance before you get rooted to that spot." He started to guide her out on the floor. "Here. Leave the jacket with Ben so you can dance better."

She slipped out of the garment and handed it over. Ben nodded as he took it and left it on a bar stool next to him.

They started a two-step, Coop's hand light on her back as he guided her around the floor. "You haven't been saying much. Is something wrong?"

"No. I'm just afraid to say the wrong thing, something that will embarrass you. And I don't know much about the ranching."

"Well, I understand that, but when Ben asked you whether you rode, surely you could have said a bit more than, 'Coop taught me.' Anyway, you're not gonna embarrass me. What gives you that idea?"

Her mouth opened and shut. "Coop, all you ever talk about is how I embarrass you!"

"No, I do not. Anyway, it's only the feathers and weirdo clothes you used to wear that got me riled."

She puffed out a sigh. Out of the corner of her eye, she caught Sheila shunting on to the barstool and shuffling into Coop's denim jacket, and she wondered whether she would ever get it back. "Sheila's got your jacket on."

He glanced over. "Maybe she's cold. She'll give it back, if that's what's worrying you."

At the end of the dance, they strolled back to the other couple.

"Stole your jacket," Sheila said. "You want it back?"

"No, that's okay," Cassie muttered. "It's Coop's anyway."

Sheila laughed. "Well, I can see that, but I thought maybe you were cold or something. Sure is a chilly night. Think the weather's changing."

"Bite your dang tongue," Ben chimed in. "We've had a real good summer so far, didn't we, Coop. Don't need for it to end too soon."

"Oh, don't you guys start talking weather and cattle again, for chrissake." Sheila took a sip of her beer and glanced back at Cassie. "I hear you got a garden going. Real green thumb, someone said."

Coop put his arm around her. "Oh, hell, she's growing more things than they got in the dang grocer's—and stuffing me with more greens than I've ate in the whole past twenty years."

Sheila smiled. "You ever thought of having a stand outside the ranch? Like a farm stand they sometimes do?"

Cassie turned and looked at Coop to see his reaction to that. It might be a good source of income, however small. "I think it might be a bit dicey…"

"You gotta speak up here," Ben butted in. "With all this noise, you'll never make yourself heard with a mousy voice like that."

The other three laughed a bit and she tried speaking louder. "I said it might be a bit dicey. Coop says the weather can turn any day."

"Well." Ben tapped a cigarette out of his pack and lit it, handed it to Sheila, and then did the same for himself. "That's true. But then, nothing ventured, nothing gained. Whatever you grow, whatever you sell, is more than what you had before."

"That's true, sweetheart." Coop turned to her. "But I'm not sure I want you standing on the road all day long."

She blinked. It was the first time Coop had called her "sweetheart," and she caught the exchange of glances between Ben and Sheila. It was his sudden possessiveness, she figured, that had them amused. According to Mrs. Craven, no one in the area could figure what, exactly, was going on between them. Was she so different from them all it couldn't be considered a long-term relationship? Or was she so much younger than Coop that it struck them all as odd? At times she certainly felt younger than him, yet by the same token, she felt as if she were suddenly a whole lot older than her former friends. But girls from college were already married, having babies, settled down. She had opted to head off on an adventure and ended up living with this man in the wilds of Wyoming. She couldn't figure herself what was happening in her life.

"In Massachusetts, I often see farm stands on an honor system. Like, they leave a bunch of vegetables out on a stand with something like a large jar for the money, a sign that says what they'd expect to be paid for each item. And they go collect the cash at the end of the day or whenever." She got excited explaining this, as the idea took hold in her mind. "I mean, if someone takes the stuff and doesn't leave any money, I figure it's because they couldn't really afford it anyway, don't you think?"

There was silence for a moment as the other three looked at each other. The jukebox had come on as the band took a break, and she recognized Willie Nelson's reedy voice in the background singing about blue eyes.

She watched as Sheila blew a plume of cigarette smoke into the air like some chimneystack. Finally, Sheila said, "Well, that's a right nice idea, Cassie. If you don't mind losing some of your produce and not being paid for it, you could surely try it out, couldn't she, Coop?"

"Anything's worth a try," he said.

****

Five rounds down, Cassie felt woozy, and she certainly needed the bathroom. She looked around, spotted a line of women waiting, and excused herself to join the line. It was slow to move, probably only one stall or something, she figured, while the men came and went at a reasonable speed. Ty came by, stopped to look down at her without a word before he marched off and ignored her completely on his way back. She tried to see if he had joined Coop and Ben, but there were too many people milling about in front of their spot, blocking her view, and she couldn't make out what was happening. The hall had got very packed in the last hour or so.

When she finished, she headed in the general direction of where she thought she had left the others, then spotted Sheila talking to someone else Cassie didn't know, and Ben had moved to another group of men. Coop was nowhere to be seen until someone kicking the jukebox near the door got her attention and she spied Coop come in, arm around another woman, the denim jacket now on this girl. Uncertain what to do, she watched as they joined the group with Ty.

Marianne. It had to be.

Someone bumped into Cassie, and she peered up. Another cowboy. He touched the brim of his hat to apologize and moved on. She stood there in the middle of a mass of strangers, all shunting around, joining others, going off to dance, heading for the bar, glancing her way and moving on. She took a deep breath and snaked through the crowd to Coop. She stood behind the woman in the jacket, waited for a break when she might get Coop's attention, but she had to give up. Either he was aware of her presence and ignored her or he didn't realize she was there. At last she tapped him on the arm, and he glanced at her before he turned back to the group, laughed at something someone said, and then pivoted back to her, brows raised in question.

"Can I have the key to the truck, please? I'll wait for you there." She couldn't keep the irritated tone out of her voice.

He reached into his pocket, but then said, "You'll be waiting a long time. I'm talking here to my friends. Stay."

She gasped in a breath, felt bolder. "Well, maybe one of your friends—Ty, perhaps?—will give you a ride back so I can take the truck and go home."

At this, the woman he had his arm around turned her head, examined Cassie top to toe, and turned back. "*Home*?" she muttered to Coop.

Cooper grimaced. "Have another drink, Cass. Here's some cash. Place closes at ten anyways."

"I don't want another drink. I'll wait in the truck if none of your friends can drop you off."

He let go of the woman she believed to be Marianne and faced Cassie, annoyance written all over him. "You can't wait in the dang truck. You'll freeze to death unless you keep the motor running for heat; Marianne's got your jacket for the moment."

So it *was* Marianne, who now flicked a smirk in

Cassie's direction. "You want it back? I can manage, Coop." And she towed off the sleeves and handed the jacket back to Cassie.

"Thanks." She shuffled into it, her eyes set on Cooper's the whole time. "I'll wait in the truck, then." She straightened up and squinted at him. "You take your time, Cooper *dear*." The sarcasm hung there as she snatched the keys from his hand and marched away.

A cold rain had started as she stood outside for a moment and tried to remember where they had parked. There were so many more trucks and cars now, and all parked haphazardly. She figured they all must leave about the same time, early to bed after the ten o'clock closing, back up at five as usual. She stretched the jacket up over her head to try to give herself some shelter and started to ramble through the lot, glancing this way and that to look for the pickup. The rain came down a bit heavier now, and at last she spotted Cooper's truck—black, with a bent rear bumper where some horse had kicked it, so he said. Hardly able to see what she was doing in the dark, with rivulets of rain making their way down her face as she struggled to get the key in the lock, she pulled the door open and slid into the passenger's seat. She put the key in the ignition for a minute to see the clock—nine twenty-four—then leaned against the window to wait.

A roll of thunder made her jump. Blades of lightning zigzagged in a circuit around the jagged peaks of mountains briefly lit, as if they were taking turns, followed by more thunder as the crests dissolved in anger. A few early departures thinned out the trucks, but Coop was nowhere to be seen.

It was the roar of a pickup pulling away that woke

her some time later. She stuck the key back in the ignition once more to see the clock—ten forty-five. So much for "this place closes at ten." There was now only one other truck in the lot and Cassie knew it was Ty's. Ty's and his sister's. Marianne. Resentment started to well up in her, an irritation she tried to push back, ignore, not let it hurt her. But the weariness and disappointment she now felt gained strength, and she no longer cared. She was exhausted from living in this limbo she had entered, this no-man's land of hanging on for someone who didn't seem to care for her at all one moment, then made her feel like his whole world the next. *Screw you*, she thought. *Screw you and your whole damn ranching life and Wyoming.* But she knew she didn't really mean that or even feel that. She had come to love the ranch and Wyoming and the life she had—waking to mornings of cool, crisp air, seeing the mountains beyond the curtains, and the spread of endless sky, the long roll of brush into the distance.

She got out of the passenger side to move over to the driver's seat when she heard the gales of laughter coming from the hall porch. Another flash of lightning. She tugged open the door.

"What the hell are you doing?" Coop's voice was thick with drink, and he stumbled as he came up to her, reaching out for the key.

"I'll drive. You're far too drunk to drive." She stood her ground and faced him.

"No woman is gonna drive me home like some naughty child. Give me the dang keys, Cassie."

"No."

Coop moved up to her, his breath hot with the smell of beer, and she could smell something else on him. Perfume. "You give me those damn keys, Cassie, before I bust you one. Now hand them over."

The dirt was mud now and squelched as he moved toward her, and she took a step away.

He made a grab for her and slipped but regained his balance as he steadied himself with a hand on the hood of the truck. "You give me those damn keys!"

Ty's truck pulled by and honked as it turned out onto the highway. The lights in the hall finally shut off, leaving them in total darkness. As her attention was taken by the last remaining man closing the door to lock up, Cooper snatched the keys away.

"Get in the fucking truck before I leave you here to walk, you damn bitch." His speech was slurred, but the words tumbled out with a deep venom colored by his drink.

She stood uncertain of what to do but considered her only real option for the night was to go with him. Pack up and leave tomorrow. She stood as he struggled into the driver's seat and started the engine. Then she pulled open the passenger door and slid in. The seatbelts they never used hung there, and she pulled hers across and clicked it into place as he pulled onto the highway.

Coop's head turned, and he snarled at her sudden distrust of him. "You dumb…you don't think I can drive? You know the number of times I've driven home from here after a few beers?"

"You've had more than a few beers," she mumbled.

"Well, what the hell? What's got into you tonight? I took you out for a good time and all you did was ignore my friends, not join in, hardly a word spoke, and then you go off for hours and leave me."

"*Leave you?* I went to the goddamn ladies' room. What? I'm not allowed to go to the bathroom now?"

"'Course you are, but when you came back, you just stood there like some bimbo."

"Don't give me that. You reek of her perfume. You were all over her. For all I know you were screwing her all this time!"

Cooper's open palm came off the steering wheel toward her face. She jerked away, out of reach and, as she did so, shouted, "Watch out!"

The truck hit something, throwing both of them sideways. It lurched and bumped, then veered off the road into the soft shoulder and came to a stop. Coop was breathing heavily, both hands now on the wheel as if glued there. He leaned forward and rested his head on the cool metal before rubbing his neck as outside a moose scampered away. "Well, that was…" He glanced over to her, a trickle of blood coming out of the corner of her mouth, her head lolled against the window.

She shut her eyes.

"Jesus, no! Cassie! Cassie!" He tried to get across the shift to reach her, to touch her face.

"Don't you dare touch me. Don't you dare." Still stunned, she hefted in a quavering breath, sinking into the corner.

He sat back in his seat and stared at her. "Jesus, I thought you were dead. Should I take you to the hospital?"

"I'm fine," she snarled back at him. "I bit my cheek and my lip. Just take me the hell back to the ranch for now."

For several minutes, Coop just sat there while she

kept her eyes shut, unmoving. Eventually she heard the truck cough and sputter and come back to life, the whirl of the wheels as they at last spit their way out of the mud and onto the road.

At the house, he sat there in the truck in silence before he got out. He came around to open the door for her, but she just sat still. The rain was coming down again, and finally she slipped out, went straight into the house and upstairs. To the guestroom. And locked the door.

Chapter Seven

"Cassie, for chrissake, come out of there already. I can see you've been sneaking down to eat while I'm out and that a few things have been done in your garden. Did you see how nice the fence looks? We're just finishing it now. Thought you'd like to come on down and see."

Silence.

Cooper hit the door with his fist and sighed. He guessed he'd really done it this time, upset her to the point she was certainly considering heading off to California. Now he'd given himself the job of winning her back. "I told you I was sorry. What more do you want? I didn't have…you know…do anything with Marianne—Ty was trying to get us back together was all, and I was telling him 'no,' and Marianne was telling him we're just good friends. And that was it. We were talking is all." He hammered the door again, but there was still no response. "Shit. If you're gonna act like this, you might as well head on out to California or something." Which he knew was not what he wanted as he started to twist away, then pivoted back. "Not that I want you to go—I want to make that clear. I miss your dang cooking. You don't want me eating nothing but steak all the time, do you?"

Silence.

"Shit." He paced in front of the door a few times.

How had the woman wormed her way into his life? "You're acting childish now, Cassie, like a spoiled child who won't accept an apology. I did have too much to drink. Is that what you want me to say? But there are always moose and elk and wildlife hereabouts, and that could have happened to anyone. I warned you about it, didn't I? I told you to be careful driving."

No answer.

"Jesus H., Cassie, you do try a man." He waited, to no avail. "I gotta get back to work. You wanna stew in there a lifetime, you go ahead and do what you dang well please. See if I care!"

****

She had heard the discussion as they mixed cement for the fence posts they now had hammered in, the soft voice of Hank as he advised Coop, the murmur drifting up to her window during lulls in the work. She knew by now this was Coop's way of apologizing; he would always do something nice for her if he felt he had done or said something wrong. But this seesaw life she led with him, coupled with her indecisiveness about California, made her feel lost and aimless, unattached to anyone who really wanted her, while her own heart ached at the sight of him sometimes. And she loved it here, she realized with a stabbing certainty; she didn't want to live anyplace else. She liked waking to look out at the plains, the backdrop of the pinnacles, mauves and blues rising from the ocher grasses of the prairie, the cows in their steadfast postures—icons—elk and antelope running in herds. She could probably find her friends in Haight-Ashbury—an address had been scribbled on a piece of paper when they left—but was that what she really wanted now? Living with Cooper had shown her a different world, which had been her exact aim when she set out and left her parents.

Her parents.

She'd written one brief letter to say she was all right and that she had decided to stick around Jackson Hole for a while. They probably envisaged she had some waitressing job or a post in one of the national parks, not that she was living with a man some seven years older than she.

The tap of Coop's boots sounded again on the stairs and she rested back against the wall, the book she'd been reading in her lap.

"I'm going into town. Is there something you want?" The rap of a pen or pencil sounded on the door. "I'm not gonna have a drink, I'm just gonna fetch some things we seem to need from the grocer's. Cassie?" There was a spot of hopefulness in his voice that faded when there was no reply, followed by a heavy exhalation. "Cass, how the hell long you gonna keep this up? You can't stay in there forever. I'll be married with five kids and we'll have this specter or whatever living in that room we never see. How am I gonna explain that to my wife?"

She couldn't help a sputter and a snort. Still, she wouldn't relent, couldn't forgive, would hold on as long as possible deciding what to do, where to be.

"I heard that." There was a pause. "I'll let you drive if you come out."

Nothing.

She could hear another breath blown out before he marched away, then the rhythm of his descent down the steps.

A couple of hours later, she heard the truck pull

back in and pinched back a corner of the curtain to watch Coop unload. He glanced up at her window a second, and she snatched away but caught him shake his head as he glimpsed her. It wasn't long before she heard the tattoo of his boots as he marched up the stairs, but this time he didn't call through the door, just stopped and left something outside before he went back down.

Curious, she waited until she believed the coast to be clear before she slid open the lock and quietly turned the door handle to peep out. She worried if he'd brought flowers she'd need a vase and water or they'd die.

Chocolates. A huge box of chocolates.

Silly man, she thought. And closed the door again.

****

As night colored the sky, Cassie pulled open her curtain and peered out as shades of pink and purple streaked across the treetops, tinged by a blackness off to the east. Storm clouds. She could feel the sudden September chill and heard the propane heating click on as Coop entered the kitchen with the dogs whining, downstairs. He stomped off his boots for the night. She supposed he was looking after himself, just the way he had lived before she ever came on the scene, cooking whatever he liked to eat, having his beers, occasionally watching TV, Elam and Wayne at his feet, before climbing up to bed. And she supposed he realized at some point she would have to come out and start living again, either here or moving on if she couldn't forgive him.

Love, to her, had always been difficult to define. She believed it to be something deep inside, something shared, a song in your head playing constantly in the background. Always there. It was your heart skipping and your stomach somersaulting when the person walked in the room, got close. And that was what she felt for Coop now; those were her very feelings every time he got near. Even though she believed those feelings were not returned, she knew the thought of leaving him was painful. He offered her a steadfastness, a certainty, a support she hadn't experienced before, small kindnesses she enjoyed and wouldn't want to do without. And maybe that was it: she didn't like the thought of doing without him, of leaving.

Hearing sports come on the TV, she snuck out to wash for bed, still ignoring the chocolates where he'd left them. Later, she lay in bed and listened to his routine she knew so well now, the clunk of his belt buckle as his jeans hit the floor, the little hop of getting his leg in his pajama bottoms, and his stroll down to the bathroom to wash, and back again, before the light clicked off. It wasn't long before soft snores came through the wall, and Cassie realized she missed all that, the way he curled around her in that big, old bed, their feet entwined, his head nuzzled into her shoulder sometimes, the grizzle of his day's beard growth against her skin. She thought of sneaking into the bed but gave up the idea; he'd probably just throw an arm over her and fall back to sleep, say nothing except maybe, "I knew you'd come 'round."

It was a crash of thunder that woke her, followed by the sound of something like a lover throwing pebbles against the window, but this was no lover. Its power was so forceful she thought the window might break. As she pulled back the curtain, blades of lightning mapped the sky, a deep indigo when lit, the forks like veins in the sky's skin. She heard the rustle of Coop waking, the creak of him sitting up in bed. For a moment she sat watching, and then realized her garden would be decimated.

She grabbed an old shirt of his she used as a bathrobe, unlatched the door, crashed barefoot into the box of chocolates, and sent them flying and scattered all over as they fell from the hallway, through the banister, into the corridor below. She flew down the stairs. Cooper appeared as he pulled on his jeans and a shirt and followed behind her.

"Cassie, don't, don't! It's too late, and there's lightning!"

She pulled open the kitchen door and ran into the garden, fumbling with the new gate to yank it open as she tried to protect her head from the pounding hail, hail the size of her fist. Cooper had pulled on his boots and made a grab for her, but she wrenched away, unsure of what to do to save the remains of her crops.

"You're not gonna save anything now, Cass," he shouted above the maelstrom. "Give it up. Get back inside. I have to go see to the cattle!"

The dogs appeared on the path, out of the kitchen where they'd been sleeping, and set up a yowling that added to the din. Sick of seeing all her hard work in ruins, she turned and pushed past Coop, who stood helpless. She grabbed a knife from the kitchen block and came back out to cut heads of cabbage and whatever else she felt she could save. But it was no use: the hail continued to beat her, and she shivered with the cold, shaking. The shirt stuck to her lithe body until she collapsed in the mud.

"Cassie, you can't do any more. You best get inside, sweetheart. It was the end of the season anyway." He bent over her, soaked through himself, his hair plastered to his head. "Cassie?" He knelt beside her, watched helplessly as the sobs came and wracked her body, as she swayed with its pain.

He gathered her up into his arms just as Hank's pickup pulled into the yard and he and the older cowboy got out, slicker-covered, and looked on.

"We'll saddle up," the elder said, his voice drowned in the rumble of the storm. "You come on, Coop, when you can."

Coop just nodded and headed back to the house, Cassie in his arms.

****

She snuffled and sneezed through an uneasy reconciliation with him. Coop toughed it out, rejected so much as an aspirin, followed his usual routine, and performed his chores punctuated by deafening nose-blowing, which eventually became a wracking cough. She bought a bucketload of vitamin C, along with strange items she had trouble finding in town: Echinacea, zinc, propolis.

Their colds cleared about the same time a tenuous settlement occurred, so that by October, probably to be sure to win her back, Coop had reluctantly given in to her idea of buying a load of pumpkins for pies she intended to sell in town through a couple of shops.

Mrs. Craven found her in the kitchen, carving her third jack o' lantern.

"If those are for Halloween, you may as well stop right there. Cooper Byrnes will never let a bunch of kids come marching up to his door. Never has, never will. Just like his daddy before him."

"Why not?" She held the knife in midair but soon continued to slash out triangle eyes.

"Why not? *Why not?* Good heavens, girl, you been living with the man these near on six months, pretending you're sleeping alone in the guest room, and you stand there thinking he celebrates Halloween?"

"He doesn't have to celebrate Halloween. I do."

"Well, there ain't nobody gonna come up your drive to the house, jump out, say trick or treat, grab candies, and go off again on their merry way. That much I can tell you."

"Because it's too far or because of Coop?" *He isn't that scary!*

Mrs. Craven heaved a sigh and leaned back against the worktop, watching Cassie push out the nose. "A little of both, I reckon. Some of the parents around here drive the kids about, but they all know Coop is single and doesn't do nothing for them so there's no real reason to come on up."

She attempted to think of a way to say Cooper was no longer single, but it appeared, as far as anyone else was concerned, she didn't count. "Well, maybe I'll make a sign with an arrow on the road, by the gate."

"You'd do better to please him by maybe selling those lanterns. Put one out on a crate by the gate with a sign saying lanterns for sale. That's what I'd do."

Cassie looked up and smiled. "Good idea. Maybe it is too much to expect trick-or-treaters to come all this way up to the house."

"I'd say." Mrs. Craven put a hand to her hip and watched her for a few moments before grabbing a dishtowel and wiping some plates in the rack. "You are a weird couple, you with your cooking and gardening and college degree, wearing your heart on your sleeve—"

"I don't wear my heart on my sleeve."

"No, everything is written all over your face. You're like some great big puppy wagging its tail and trying to get a morsel from that man, and he's about as giving as a headstone on a grave."

She snorted a laugh. "Well. I'm beginning to understand him better after all this time. We have a working relationship."

"Yeah, but, you at your age, you want a little lovin', a little more than a 'working relationship.' And Cooper being the product of two of the most tight-lipped, harsh, cold-blooded parents there could be, he's not ever gonna change."

Cassie held the finished pumpkin out to admire and tried to seem disinterested. "What were—I guess *are*, as his mother's still alive, isn't she?—what are they like? Did you know them well?"

Mrs. Craven hung the dishtowel on the oven rail and took a beat to smooth it out. "Well, I guess I knew them about as well as anyone hereabout. Worked for them twenty years or so. His daddy was all right with me and others, but he was one of these hard-bitten men, thought 'his way or the highway' all the time, tried to instill in Cooper a sense of the value of the ranch—oh, not in money terms, ya know, but as his inheritance, land. Land and cattle, that's all that man knew. I never saw him once praise the boy, even when he came in with trophies from 4H or FFA. Then Coop won a scholarship to go on to agricultural college, and Byrnes nixed that. Told him he was learning everything he needed to know right here."

Cassie placed the pumpkin on the kitchen table, where the assorted group had different faces. She stood back and admired her handiwork, one with a huge smile and round eyes, another looking positively evil, the third with a lopsided grin. She took up another, pulled a clean bowl over for the pulp and seeds, and started cutting the lid. "What is his mother like, then?"

"Oh, mean bitch. You haven't met her yet?"

"No. Coop goes over to his sister's on his own."

"Well, then he's protecting you from her, I'd say. How the sister turned out so sweet and good is beyond me. 'Course, she did go and get herself hitched real young, got away from her daddy and mama quick as she could. Then she goes and takes her mother in. Beats me. But you want to stay well away from that one, his mother." She crossed her arms as if protecting herself from the woman. "I don't know if Byrnes changed her with his lack of love or she was always that way, but she was worse than he was. Heartless is what she is."

"Well." She struggled to get the knife around, her hand now aching. "I guess I never will—"

The door banged open and Coop marched in, a smile on his face, which vanished when he spotted the pumpkin lanterns. "What are you doing? You said those dang pumpkins were for pies to sell."

She stood, the knife poised in her hand as she studied him. "Well, I had more than enough pumpkin for pies, and there's no point in wasting the remaining shells. I thought I could sell the jack o' lanterns as well. Maybe put them on a crate by the road or something?"

"Hmm." Coop stood there, his mouth puckered in thought. "I guess that'll be all right." He sauntered off to the small room he called his office, next to the kitchen.

She exchanged glances with Mrs. Craven, each getting on with their chores when Cooper reappeared, two rifles in his arms.

She stood back and looked at them. "Where…where are you going with those?"

"Hunting, of course. Dusty and I—"

Cassie grimaced. "Who's Dusty?"

"Oh, Cassie. You know Dusty. The older puncher who works here. Jeez, how long you been livin' here?"

"So what are you hunting?"

Mrs. Craven coughed.

"I'm hunting my dinner, of course, just like the cave men," Coop snarled. "You got a problem with that?"

"You're going to *kill* things?"

Coop glanced over at the finished pumpkins and, for a terrible moment, she thought he was going to bring the rifles down on them.

He switched back to her. "Listen to me," he said in a low, steady voice. "If I don't hunt, that wildlife eats my cattle's feed, grazes my cattle's land, drinks my cattle's water. I don't kill anything that don't need killing here. You have a coyote in the henhouse, you think you just let him be? This is the way it is on a ranch: the land and the cattle come first. Always have, always will, and no little city girl is gonna tell me how to live. You got that?"

She blinked back tears and took the knife to her pumpkin with renewed vigor.

"I asked you a question."

"I—"

"And anyways, I eat most of what I take, or share it out. Some folks like meat, you know."

"Those pumpkins will make great pies for Thanksgiving, won't they, Coop?" Mrs. Craven chimed in before the argument took a turn for any worse.

He regarded her as if noticing she was present for the first time, then started for the door.

With a slight note of mischievousness, Mrs. Craven asked, "You taking Cassie to Sunny's for Thanksgiving?"

Cooper stopped in his tracks. He spoke to the door without turning back. "I haven't thought about Thanksgiving with my sister. Maybe we'll just have it here, have Sheila and Ben over or tie up with them. That would be better than trekking all the way over to Sheridan, probably getting stuck in a snowstorm or something. Anyway," he said, pivoting back with a smile, "Way Cassie cooks, the meal would be far better at home."

"Turkey's a bit large for just the two or even four of you."

"Well, I'm sure that chest freezer I went and bought is good for something."

The screen slammed shut behind him before the truck roared away.

Chapter Eight

Snow muffled the farewells to Ben and Sheila, who wrapped her arms about herself, after she gave Cassie a hug, and disappeared back into the house. Coop's hands were filled with the washed-out bowls and dishes of items they had brought to contribute to the Thanksgiving dinner, but he stuck out his elbow for Cassie to hold as they gingerly made their way over the ice to the truck. Inside, she rubbed her hands together, hunched against the chill, and waited for him to get the heater going.

"Put that seatbelt on, will ya? With icy roads, you never know what will happen." His glance skimmed toward her before he turned the key, yanked on his own seatbelt, and drove off.

He waited for her to make a reference to what *had* happened not so long ago, but she only shivered and clasped her mittened hands to her chest. "Can we have the heat on? Please."

"Engine's gotta warm up. Give it a sec." He stole another glance. "You plannin' on going to California or something? 'Cause if not, you better get a decent coat. That denim jacket of mine won't keep you warm through a Wyoming winter."

"Well. I'll see."

He wished she would say something one way or the other. He knew she had no idea what the winter would bring, how low the temperatures could drop, how the pipes could freeze up, the power go. Yet he was afraid to push the point, afraid to say any of it lest she take it as a reason to leave.

He drove through town, halos of light from the streetlamps marking the edge of the road, the deserted streets hushed, silent, not a soul to be seen. By the time he got back out onto the highway home, she was asleep, her head tucked down like a pigeon, her hands as if in prayer against her chest. He had to gather her and carry her upstairs, kicking the crabbing dogs out of the way before he gave the outside door a shove closed with his foot. He left Cassie asleep on the bed while he brought in the empty containers from the truck and fed the dogs, closed down the lights, and headed back up.

Cassie stood groggy and naked as she pulled her last sock off. He halted in the doorway, considered her as she reached for her nightdress under the pillow, but he was too quick for her. He seized her hand.

"Don't," was all he said. He pushed her headband off and smoothed her hair down with a gentle hand, ran his fingers through it, then pulled her into him, teased her lips with his before he captured her mouth and lowered her with care onto the bed.

Cassie knew every inch of Coop's body now, loved his body—the smooth bulge of the muscle of his upper arms, the callous of his hands, the flat hard chest as he lowered himself onto her. She felt the dense curls of his hair as she gripped him closer, and ran one finger down the gully of that scar above his eye. She wanted him; she wanted that sense of fulfillment when he moved within her, his soft moans, his deep breaths. But more than anything, she wanted to hear his words, three little words that never came, however he acted. *Say it*, she thought. *Just say it! Once! That's all I need. Just fucking say it once!*

In the morning, entwined under the mountain of covers, he rubbed his nose against her before he kissed her once more. His lips parted as if he were going to say something, but then he just pecked her on the cheek one more time and hopped over her.

She watched as he pulled on his jeans.

Coop twisted toward her. "You on the dang pill yet?"

"No. They don't like giving it to unmarried women."

"Well...you better get on the damn pill, Cass. We've forgotten more than once now, and we sure as heck don't want any accidents."

****

She sat at the kitchen table, seed catalogs Coop had brought from the hardware shop spread out in front of her. Their abundant flowers spewed colors in stark contrast to the solemn white world outside the window, where a long tunnel of cloud hung low on the distant horizon. The dogs slept at her feet as the chained tires on the tractor growled with one of the men clearing the drive. She had a pen and paper to list what she thought might grow here, if the damn snow ever melted. With several months to get through yet, she had no idea if or when she could plant again, or what she could do in the interim.

Christmas presents. That was going to be tough. What little money she'd earned wouldn't stretch very far, and she'd found a large box hidden away in Coop's closet that might well be for her, though she wouldn't dare open it. A couple of weeks ago he'd bought himself a new hat, and she considered doing a beaded hatband on the little loom she now had, but she thought he'd find it too fancy for his taste. And then she had an idea.

A truck pulled up outside, and the horn was honked, followed by the slam of the door. *Ty.*

She gathered up the seed catalogs and screeched back the dinette chair, disturbing the dogs, who left for the fire in the living room, their claws clicking on the linoleum.

It was too late.

"Well, lookee, lookee, who have we here?" Ty stood in the doorway, stomped snow from his boots and slammed the door shut behind him. "You still here? I woulda thought California would be more appealing this time of year. That was your intention, wasn't it? San Francisco, I seem to remember."

She stood, the catalogs against her chest as if they might provide some protection from his tirade.

"What do ya got there, Cassie?" He yanked them out of her hands. "Well, I'll be. Looks like you might be planning on staying a spell, huh? I mean, if you're gonna plant flowers and vegetables, that would have to be May, most likely, and then you'd want to stick around to watch them grow, and then you'd surely want to harvest them, wouldn't you?"

She didn't reply, but reached out for their return. Ty held them out of her reach.

"Cat got your tongue? Why the hell don't you just move on? Shove off. What the hell are you doing here anyway? Why don't you leave Coop alone, stop hanging on and living off him, let him get on with his life."

"Maybe Coop likes me here." She reached to pluck the catalogs back, but Ty still held them high. She found him offensive, a world away from Coop, as tough as Coop could be. Ty was in another category altogether, and she both hated and feared him.

"Yeah, I bet he does." Ty's voice was a nasty, insinuating mutter. "You must be the best damn fuck around."

She shook her head in disgust and tried once more to grasp the catalogs. Ty threw them on the table behind her and gripped her shoulders hard.

"That's the pretty little blouse you wore the first night he saw you, those mirrored things on it. I wonder what's under that blouse. You wear a bra?" He shoved her hard onto the table, sent the catalogs flying as she struggled to get up. He yanked at the blouse from the open neckline down. His action revealed her camisole underneath, but it wouldn't tear.

"You know we've often shared women? Did you know that?" His breath came hot into her face as his hand reached between her legs, and she struggled to twist away.

The stench of meat mixed with coffee met her nostrils.

"Let's just see if you wear any panties. You wear one of them sexy G-strings like the strippers do?"

She coiled against him, trying to get her right leg over and force Ty's hand away. He had his other hand near her throat, but she spat in his face. An attempt at head-butting him knocked his hat to the floor.

Ty yanked back, his right hand coming down with a hard blow to her head while his left fumbled with the zipper on her jeans. "Bitch! You think Coop is gonna come and save you? You think he even cares? Think again, sweetheart. He's way out with the herd."

Cassie managed to get a knee up and attempted a kick at Ty, but it was no use. The dogs came back in and started yowling and barking, but Ty paid them no mind. He tugged at her jeans until he got them part way down, but suddenly, with a gust of icy air, Mrs. Craven was in the room. She pulled a knife from the block just as Hank entered behind her.

"You sonuvabitch!" Hank pushed Ty off the table and sent him flying against the far wall.

Ty lost his balance and slid down.

And then Cooper came in. "What…what the hell?"

She struggled to stand and get her jeans back up, a line of mucus and tears trailed down her face as she sniffled.

Mrs. Craven stood stock still, as if frozen to the spot, the knife in her hand.

Hank jerked up Ty by his shirt collar, then shoved him back against the wall once more. "That's your friend, Coop, that animal there." He dusted down his hands and slouched his coat back into position before he ambled past Mrs. Craven, picked up his own hat from the floor, and nodded to Cassie.

She stood granite-still, her arms wrapped around herself, head bent.

Cooper closed the door behind Hank. His face was like stone, deep ruts of anger etched into the brackets around his mouth. "Ty, what the hell were you doing?"

Ty ran a hand along his lip and looked at the blood it brought up. "You don't care about that bitch. You—"

"*What?*" Coop shook his head as if he needed to

decipher to himself what Ty had said. He sucked in a breath. "I don't care about her? What the hell do you know about my feelings? What business is it of yours? Ty, you and I been friends these twenty years or so, been to school together, been to high school together, watched each other's back—"

"That's right—" Ty started.

"Shut up! Now you get the hell out of here, and don't you ever set foot on my land again, you hear me? I don't want to see your face within a mile of that girl." He waited while no one moved. "Well, go on! Get out!"

Ty scrambled to his feet as Mrs. Craven waved the knife in his direction. He scooped up his hat as he tripped to the door. When it slammed behind him, Cassie started to sob. The dogs set up their own wailing. The screech of tires on the ice signaled Ty's departure.

Coop sighed and gathered up the catalogs, then tossed them back on the table. He held her to his chest for a moment. "Geesh, Cassie, why didn't you shout?"

****

A picture postcard scene of white hills against the gray sky, strokes of clouds like strands of white thread, greeted Cassie as she pulled back the bedroom curtain. Coop stood in the doorway, hand on hip. As she peered across at him, he grimaced.

"Bad enough drive on a good day, some six hours to Sheridan. Most of the roads I normally take may be closed. It'll be a hellish drive."

She bit her lip. "Well, whatever you decide is fine by me. I think I could still get something from the grocer's to cook up for Christmas, if you want to stay here. You could always go on after, when the roads clear."

Coop scowled. He tapped his boot nervously as if it were the cogs of his brain making its decision. "Nope," he said as he turned, but he swiveled back to her. "You packed? You got some overnight things together?"

She studied her hands. "You're sure you want me to go?"

"For chrissake, woman, I can hardly leave you here for Christmas on your own. And Hank's got the dogs already. Dusty and him are gonna look after things for me. What'll they think if I up and leave you on your own? I'll never hear the end of it."

She looked at him. *Well, Merry Christmas to you, too, pal.* "I could say I didn't feel well enough, that I was ill."

"Nope." He softened a bit. "I go, you go." He hesitated. "Go on, get your stuff together. I'm gonna start loading the truck before nightfall." He bent into the closet where he'd kept the presents and started pulling them out, the large box she thought was for her among them. "I'm not gonna bother bringing your gift along; we can exchange—if there be an exchange— when we get back home." He pivoted on his knees to look at her. "What are you so dang worried about? I'm not expecting much. I know you don't have much money."

She got up and headed to the door. "No."

"No what?"

"No, I'm afraid I hadn't much money."

"Well, then."

She stepped into the guest room where her satchel was and got some things together—a change of underwear, a cardigan. Nothing she owned seemed right to wear to meet Cooper's mother, after what Mrs. Craven had said. She shook out a velvet skirt she thought might do for Christmas dinner, then thought of telling Coop she really felt ill. Out in the yard, he was checking the chains on the truck, pulling the tarpaulin over the load bed, his collar up against the wind. *Handsome bastard.* Ice crystals were forming on the window as she peeped out, a frozen version of the veins on a leaf. She wondered if they would make it to Sheridan.

She heard him come in and stomp snow off his boots before he tramped upstairs.

"I'm thinking we might be safer going via Dubois and up, but that'll take ages, and a night in a motel."

She faced him, smoothing out a blouse before stuffing it into the satchel. "Well, don't ask me. How would I know?"

"I'm not asking. I'm just sayin', thinking out loud." He started out the door, then spun back. "You're not wearing any of that hippie stuff, are you?"

She heaved a sigh. "No. I'm not wearing any 'hippie stuff.' But I don't have a lot to choose from, either."

"Well. Do the best you can. We'll get an early night and head off at 5:30."

This would be the first time she was meeting his family and, after what Mrs. Craven had told her, she didn't look forward to meeting his mother. She guessed he was nervous too, and she guessed it had to be done. After all, they'd been living together for months now, and the mother must know about it if Coop was bringing Cassie along. She would've felt a whole lot better if they'd invited Sunny and the family down here, but Coop didn't particularly like having the kids in his home, he'd said; they got bored easily and then made a nuisance of themselves. So they were going, and what could go wrong, really, when you came down to it. At Christmas.

****

They woke to clear, starlit skies, the Milky Way a vanilla smudge across the indigo darkness. Coop's lips stretched in a momentary smile before he pinched them together again, glancing at her. "Looks like the storm missed us. I think I can try the normal route."

He insisted on doing all the driving, telling her she had no experience on snow and ice and probably wouldn't stay awake anyway. "You been taking so many naps lately, Cass. You really ought to go see the doctor, the woman's doc—what's it called? The gynecologist? Maybe you need some iron pills or something. And you sure as hell need the pill. What's the use of there being a birth control pill if I still have to use sheaths?"

She drew a face in the frost on the window. "I made an appointment with a doctor over in Idaho Falls—"

"That's down the dang Teton Pass, Cass. I told you I didn't want you driving that in winter." He slammed the steering wheel, worry mixed with annoyance.

"Well, I thought it was better than going to a doctor in Jackson and maybe having the whole town know about it."

"The whole dang town knows anyway," he mumbled. "You think people still believe you're sleeping in the guest room?"

"Noooo. But…"

He glanced across at her and tried to suppress a smile. "I got this woman living with me for seven months, but we're just good friends, huh?"

She rested her elbow on the chill of the window ledge and nestled her head in her hand.

He wondered what they were as a couple, exactly, whether she would stay, what had happened about her California plans.

Outside, daybreak let a watery yellow sun trim treetops that suddenly loomed out of the dark, the occasional ranch house in the distance, fences just visible through the snow.

"I'm going to Idaho Falls, Coop." Her voice was steady, brokered no argument. "I've made the appointment, and I just don't want to go to some local I'm bound to bump into somewhere, sometime."

"Ranching community and doctors don't mix much. Not likely."

"I don't care."

"I'm gonna have to take time off, then, to drive you, 'cause you sure as hell aren't doing that drive on your own. That means probably paying Hank or Dusty extra time or something."

He glanced over at her as she turned and leaned against the door as much as the seatbelt would permit. "No, Coop. Stop treating me like a child. You're not gonna take time off, and I *am* gonna do the drive, and it'll be fine."

"My truck, my say."

"*Coop!*"

He swiveled toward her and peered at her, and he finally took in the determination written on her face. It struck him with the force of a baton blow that she had changed, how she had transformed over the last months, how she had made a niche for herself on the ranch, found a routine of usefulness, and looked after him, even. Grown up. "Fine. Have it your way. You come back with your tail between your legs 'cause you went and had a wreck—"

"Ugh!" Cassie covered her ears with her hands.

He laughed. "Okay." He kept his voice low so she could hardly hear him.

"What did you say?"

"Okay. Okay. I said okay. Have it your way, then."

Chapter Nine

Sunny's family home was a Victorian clapboard on a large plot on the Sheridan outskirts. Her husband, a local lawyer, was out when they arrived, taking gifts to some friends and doing a round of visits, while Sunny had stayed with her mother to await their arrival. As she greeted them, Cassie began to relax. The sound of children playing came from an upstairs room, and the television blared from somewhere off down a hallway. It seemed so normal and homey.

"I'm so pleased to meet ya at long last," Sunny said, taking the denim jacket Cassie had worn again. "Goodness, is this all ya had on? You must have froze to death. Cooper, what the hell's wrong with you, letting her come out in that?"

"I been at her for weeks now, saying she had to get herself a coat," he replied. He dropped his hat on a peg by the door.

An air of nervousness emanated from both siblings, an electric hum between them.

She just smiled. "I was fine. The heat in the truck is sufficient. We get really cold winters in Boston as well, and I used to love to walk out in them, in blizzards, even."

"Oh! Is that where you're from? Boston?" Sunny started to lead them into the kitchen. "Cooper didn't say."

"Yes, I did. I thought I did."

She looked at him, then at his sister, noting the resemblance. She wondered where their mother was. "This house is lovely."

"But not so nice as the ranch house, is it? I loved growing up on the ranch."

"Yes. I suppose the ranch is a great place for kids to grow up."

Cooper cleared his throat.

"Well, 'course we had our chores before and after school and weekends and all, but we both loved 4H, didn't we, Coop? You have anything like that back east?"

"Uh…Brownies?"

Coop snorted. "I don't think it's quite the same."

"Oh, Cooper. Don't you pay him no mind, now, ya hear? Ya give him a rope to hang himself, he'll complain about the quality of it. But I suspect you know all that by now." Sunny reached in a cupboard for three mugs. "Coffee? Or you ready for something stronger?"

"I'll have a beer, Sunny. After that drive, I think I deserve one."

Or did he need one? His apparent jitters made her nervous once more.

"You come up via Cody, then? Road wasn't closed?"

"Down to one lane. Slow going." He snapped open the can Sunny handed him.

Cassie took the coffee she was offered, wondering if she'd sleep with the caffeine.

There seemed to be an invisible wire between the two siblings, a wire that was taut with nervous tension, sparking as if there were a short circuit.

"So where's Mama, then? She watching game shows again?" Coop held the can to his lips, slugged it back, and tapped the counter with his free hand.

Sunny sighed and leaned back against the worktop, her own mug of coffee in hand. She looked into it for a moment. "Oh, you know, Coop. She…she's really big on watching those things."

"Well, I better start bringing things in from the truck." He crushed the empty can in his hand. "Things'll freeze to the bed before long, and Cassie's gone and baked you a pie."

"You can just leave them where they are," said a voice from the door.

Cassie warmed her hand on her mug and looked across. A woman pulled a long nubby cardigan about her and retied the belt. She had shoulder-length, wavy hair, streaks of gray like skunk markings through it, a face wrinkled into a permanent scowl.

"Oh, now, Mama." Sunny set her coffee on the counter. "You don't mean that. We've been through this sev—"

"Don't you go telling me what I do or do not mean. Cooper, you take your dang whore and get on out of here with that. She's not welcome in this house."

"Mama!" Sunny put her arm around Cassie. "This isn't your house to say so. It's Teddy's and mine, and I've invited Cassie, and she stays."

Cassie glanced at Sunny over her shoulder, then faced her opponent. "It's all right. Really it is. I told Coop I'd be fine on my own—"

"Well, there ya go," Mrs. Byrnes spat out. A drop of spittle stuck to her lower lip.

"No," Sunny started, but the two younger women caught the nod of Coop's head toward the stairs. She gave Cassie a little pat and said, "You come on upstairs now and meet my babies. Cooper and Mama need to talk."

She followed Sunny up the stairs, glanced back at Coop, who had a face like chiseled rock—*He could pose for Mount Rushmore*—although his eyes were soft when he peered her way.

The three children sat around a board game, throwing dice and moving pieces, occasionally whooping out a cry when something particularly good or maybe bad happened.

They ignored the introductions Sunny made, but Cassie paid more attention to the conversation below, clearly audible as it drifted up from the kitchen.

"You dare to bring that woman to this house, where I'm staying, a decent God-fearing Christian, and you think I'm gonna celebrate Christmas with her?"

She almost laughed at those words. She'd never thought of herself as an untouchable, a pariah. She knew some of Coop's friends and neighbors were startled by the situation, but no one had ever said anything outright or had ever called her names—at least not to her face.

"Mama, that woman's living with me, and as long as she's under my roof—"

"Well, she's not under your roof, Cooper. She's here where I'm living, and I'm not sitting down to table with some floozy you picked up in a dancehall. It's disgusting what you're doing, taking her places, being seen in public—don't you think I don't know—living with her under your roof like man and wife."

"For pity's sake, Mama, you know dang well no man now is saving himself for marriage these days. That's about the most ridiculous—"

"Don't you start talking to me like that! Men are different. Men got their needs. But a woman got to keep herself for one man."

"And that's pretty much…"

Sunny reached to close the playroom door as Cassie leaned against the wall to listen to every word floating up from below. She stayed Sunny's hand.

"I don't want the children listening," Sunny whispered.

She nodded her head in compliance and moved out into the hall. Sunny followed behind and pulled the children's door closed.

"You gonna marry that whore, then?"

"Jesus, Mama," Cooper snarled.

"Don't you take the Lord's name in vain with me!"

There was a silence. She envisaged Coop shaking his head, or going for a beer, but then she heard the sound of his hand slamming the counter.

"I asked you a question, Cooper Byrnes."

"You talk like a Christian, but you sure as hell don't act like one. I bring you my…my—"

There was the sound of a slap.

"Your whore! Say it, Cooper! I don't hear wedding bells being rung. Are you gonna marry that woman?"

Silence was followed by the question being repeated, "Are you going to marry that whore?"

Coop sighed. "No, Mama, I'm not going to marry her. But I am taking her away from here."

She exchanged a quick glance with Sunny as Coop appeared at the bottom of the stairs.

"Cassie, get your coat."

She watched as he lifted his hat from the peg, then reached into the hall closet for his own coat and the denim jacket she had worn. He looked up at her, expressionless, as she came down the stairs. Sunny stayed at the top.

"Sunny, I'm sorry 'bout this," he mumbled. "I'm not leaving Cassie on her own for Christmas. That's about as mean as a person gets."

She swiveled to look up into the dark at the top of the stairs, where Sunny nodded she understood.

"What are you going to do, Coop?" His sister's voice was soft, sorry, apologetic.

He helped Cassie into the jacket as if she were a child and took her hand. "We'll stay in a motel for the night, head on back tomorrow."

"But tomorrow's Christmas!"

"Well." Coop swung open the door. "I guess they don't close roads Christmas Day."

She gave Sunny a last glance. "It was nice meeting you," she called before he closed the door behind her.

She followed Coop down the path to the truck.

"You get in. I'm gonna take in those presents so at least they have that. Switch the ignition on so you got the heat when it comes up."

She took the key from him and turned it in the ignition, huddling into herself to stay warm. In the rearview mirror she could see Coop gather up a load of boxes and then trudge back up the path just as a station wagon pulled up behind. A hefty man got out, bundled up in woolen hat, parka, gloves, and boots, and Coop waited for him. They exchanged words for several moments before Coop handed him the presents and came back down the path, leaving the other man peering over the top of the gifts before he turned and went into the house.

Coop jerked open the driver's door and slid in, nodded to her, and pulled away.

She sat huddled into herself, and turned to the side window.

****

The motel room stank of stale smoke and dried sweat; laminate furniture dotted the dirty carpet. Coop almost jumped on one of the queen beds, his hat and boots still on, his hands locked behind his head as he tilted his Stetson forward. Cassie dropped her satchel on the other bed, the one closest to the bathroom, removed her jacket, and started to fumble in the bag. She didn't say a word, nor did Coop, but after a few moments he jumped up to turn on the TV before dropping his hat on a corner of the bed and lying back down.

"We're bombing the shit outta Hanoi, apparently. Did you hear? Or you just don't care?"

She pulled out her toiletries bag. "Why do you think America has the right to intervene in the wars of other countries?"

Coop glanced at her and sighed. "Oh, here we go again, you with your airy-fairy ideas. Don't you know we're keeping America safe? For chrissake, Cass, think about it."

"I do think about it. I think about it every day I turn on the radio and hear the name of another American killed in Viet Nam." She paused and shook her head. "I'm getting ready for bed."

"Don't you want dinner? I chose this place because

it has that restaurant. We could walk over and get us something to eat. I'm famished."

"You go." She picked up the toiletries bag and headed into the bathroom. Inside her, she knew he'd been kind, very kind for Coop, denying himself Christmas with his family to be with her instead. He really hadn't done a thing wrong. Yet weariness and his words to his mother made her feel unwanted, an outcast, and she suddenly realized she had no idea what she was doing here with him, why she had stayed on so long. She hadn't thought of the possibility of marrying him, of having his kids, but she knew there had to come a point at which the relationship would go forward, develop, or it would end. And she wasn't ready for that decision quite yet.

"Sounds like I'm gonna be eating cold pumpkin pie for my dinner," he said as the bathroom door shut. A bit louder he called, "Don't you want something to eat at all?"

She didn't answer; she let the water run until she reemerged. She dropped her toiletries bag on the bed and searched for her nightdress in the satchel.

"I asked if you didn't want something to eat."

"No. Nothing. I'm exhausted after that drive, and—"

"Well, you didn't drive!"

"No, but…" She pulled back the coverlet and then the sheet, placed the bag on the floor, and started to climb into bed.

Coop watched her. He patted a space beside him. "Why don't you come on over here. What's wrong?"

She crossed her arms against her chest and looked at him, stupefied. "I'm not sleeping with you. We both know where that leads, and you haven't brought any Durex with you."

"Well. I knew we were gonna have separate rooms at Sunny's, so… Maybe you're right. But it doesn't mean you can't cuddle for a while."

"Coop!"

"Okay. Okay." He hesitated. "How 'bout we exchange Christmas presents, then? Maybe that'll cheer you up."

"I thought you said you left mine at home. I certainly haven't brought yours."

"No, but I did." From his own satchel, he pulled out the hatband she had made for him, a wide smile on his face. A circle of intricate braiding of leather thongs an inch wide dangled from his finger.

Her anger spurted. "That was supposed to be a surprise. And it was hidden!"

"Yeah, but I found it. I was looking for that checked shirt of mine, the blue-and-white one you borrowed, and you had this hid with some things I was looking through. I didn't mean no harm, Cass. It's great. Just great." As if to prove it, he reached for his Stetson and slipped the old hatband off, replacing it with the gift. "I thought I could show it off to the family. You really have a talent, ought to go into business. Ranchers and cowboys love those braided hatbands, and quirts and riatas, too. You could have quite a little business going of custom-made—"

"I don't want a business. Maybe I'm going to California! Anyway, I'm happy with the pies and vegetables." The knowledge he was trying to be kind didn't stop her anger, her sense of being alone. As much as he'd done to spend Christmas with her, she still felt the isolation of being an outcast.

Cooper huffed out his disapproval. "Okay." He set the hat on his head for a moment, gave her a pinched smile, and then replaced the hat on the corner of the bed. "Look, I know you're upset about Mama not liking you," he started in a softer tone, "her not wanting you to stay and all, but really there was nothing I could do. She gets an idea in her head and there's no way to sway her, so it's best just to leave her be."

"I understand that." She kept her manner neutral, gave him one long look, and finally swung into bed.

"Hang on. Don't you want to know what I got you?"

"Of course. If you want me to."

"You are strange," he mumbled as he snapped open the door and went out to the truck. He returned with a large box, one she hadn't seen, and the cold pumpkin pie. "Dinner…and a gift." He held them out as if he were balancing first one, then the other.

She couldn't help but laugh.

"What would ya like first? I have one frozen pumpkin pie and one gift, somewhat chilled, no doubt, but still—"

"I'll have the gift. Please."

"Just like a woman." Coop slipped the pie onto the bedstand near him and brought her the box, perching tentatively on the side of her bed as he placed the gift in her lap. "Merry Christmas, sweetheart." He leaned in to kiss her on the cheek.

She pulled at the single ribbon that adorned the box, rolled it up to save, and lifted the lid. She parted layers of tissue paper to unveil a heavy jacket, shearling in a deep golden brown with some red embroidery on it.

She smiled widely as she pulled it out. It was quality, and must have cost a lot.

"Well? Do you like it?"

"It's really beautiful, Coop. And we both know I needed it." She looked at him, wishing so much she hadn't heard what he'd said to his mother, but her mind wouldn't cooperate by ridding her of that memory. She dropped the coat back in the box. "It's great," she said, some wistfulness in her voice. "Thanks so much."

His uncertainty was evident after the thanks that had been so automatic, so like a platitude. The lines between his brows deepened as if he were trying to figure out what he had done wrong. "I'm glad you like it," he whispered. He reached out and cupped her chin for a moment. "We'll get an early start in the morning."

****

The winter gray was just brightening as Coop turned off the highway toward Hank's place to collect the dogs, the snow going to slush on this slightly warmer day with liquid sunshine, a yolk run into the white of the egg. Fallow fields spread out on either side of the gravel lane as the truck bumped and jerked toward a small ranch house, a Christmas wreath just visible by the contrast of its green to the peeled paint on its door. Dusty's pickup was parked beside Hank's.

"Don't you think we're intruding, getting the dogs? He was going to keep them until tomorrow anyway." She pulled the new coat about her, feeling luxurious, a sense of calm pervading.

"Nah, it'll be all right. I'll just grab them, won't interfere with their celebration. You stay in the car."

The dogs started barking as soon as the motor cut. Hank opened the door, pulling Wayne back in, at the same moment Coop jumped out of the truck. The glass muffled their voices as a high wind blew, but she caught snatches of it until she rolled down the window. Coop held his hat on, and Hank's hair crossed his face in damp black fingers as he turned to glance at her in the pickup.

"I'm not taking no for an answer now, Coop. You get that girl in here. Plenty of food and always room at our table for you, you know that. Come on now. You go get Cassie and have Christmas with us. It'll be a blessing to have you both."

She could see the uncertainty in Cooper as he turned to face her. Then there was a little shake of his head as he pivoted back to Hank.

"Oh, okay, then. If you're sure. Sure beats sitting at home on our own with no dinner or nothing." There was a pause while he reconsidered, and then he just said, "Thanks." His hand went up in a beckoning gesture to her.

She opened the door, pretended she hadn't heard the conversation, and raised her brows at them both. "Merry Christmas, Hank," she called.

"You come on in here now, sweetheart." Hank gave Wayne another shove inside the house. "Maggy and me'll be right pleased to share Christmas with you both."

****

Coop leaned back at the dinner table as Cassie helped Hank's wife clear the dishes. He felt good, having had the table laughing about the partially frozen pumpkin pie he'd had for dinner the night before. He kept his eyes on Cassie, couldn't believe how she seemed to fit in with this older couple and how they welcomed her into their home, almost like a daughter—the way his mother should have done. But that hadn't happened, and for a moment he could feel himself clouding over before Hank refilled his glass.

"Did you see my new hat band? Cassie went and made it for me for Christmas, and I been telling her she ought to go into business." He got up and flipped his hat down from the peg by the door. "You see that?" There was pride in his voice.

Dusty reached out to inspect it, then handed it on to Hank. "Pretty good. Band like that'd cost you some."

"That's what I keep telling her. She could do lots of things in braid—quirts and riatas as well as bands. Could do it through the winter when she's not growing stuff."

Hank and Dusty peered over at him, both trying to hide smiles at the indication this might be a long-term view. It made him consider.

"And what does Cassie say?" Hank asked as she reappeared from the kitchen.

"About what?"

"About braiding more hat bands and riatas?"

Coop sighed and took his hat back to the pegs. "Cassie says—"

"Cassie says I don't think so. That's what Cassie says." She looked across at Coop, her hands on hips. "It's a lot of work, too slow to make a business out of it. I could take an order or two and do it, but I'm only one person; I can't do enough to keep a business going."

"Well, heck, Cass, I didn't say you should open a shop."

She collected a few more plates from the table,

stood with dishes in each hand, facing him. "I know you didn't say that. But I don't know how long I'm staying, do I, so what's the point of trying to start something?" She marched back to the kitchen.

He felt like he'd been knifed. He stood rooted to the spot, then exchanged glances with Dusty and Hank.

Dusty tilted back in his chair. "Looks like the ball is in your court, Coop."

Chapter Ten

There'd been a thaw, snow and ice leaving glistening pavement, rushing streams and creeks, gray instead of white. It apparently made Coop a little more relaxed about handing over the truck keys for her to head down Teton Pass. She drove away with him still shouting instructions on keeping it in first gear for the steep hairpin bends, not using the brakes too much, and keeping her eyes on the road through those twists and turns. She didn't know if he was more worried about his truck or her as she glanced in the rearview mirror and pulled away to Cooper's peremptory wave. He'd sauntered back toward the barns before she was out the gate.

The doctor's office was a mix of cool sanitary white and wipe-clean ozone blue plastic chairs, not particularly welcoming but comfortable enough. The staff were friendly, too—pleasant—although her stomach did somersaults when she thought about the appointment. When she asked for the birth control pill would they be disagreeable then? Disapproving? Cooper had put her on the ranch insurance for the time being—a staff member—and it made her laugh. What member of staff was she? Live-in whore? Chief cook, housekeeper, and bottlewasher? Lover to the owner? Gardener? What would Coop choose, what did he actually think of her? Was she just riding along toward a great nothing, a day when he would tell her it was time for her to move on, he'd found someone else? His words to his mother ran through her brain—*No, Mama, I'm not going to marry her.* And the *"we don't want any accidents."*

"Miss Halliday? This way, please."

She followed the slim efficiency of the nurse into a room at the end of a corridor dotted with photographs of smiling, happy babies and jubilant mothers. The woman pointed to an examining table on which lay a gown.

"Please provide a urine sample; there are cups and instructions in the bathroom out there. Then everything off and put the gown on open to the front."

She stared at her. "Everything? But I only want a prescription for—"

"You have to have a full gynecological examination for whatever you want." The nurse sniffed, and left.

Cassie closed the door. She thought of bolting now and telling Coop they wouldn't prescribe the pill, but she knew he'd only tell her to see someone else. She stared in horror at the stirrups on the end of the table but went to squeeze out a pee and handed the cup to the waiting nurse. Back in the examination room, she removed her clothing and shivered a bit as she tried to pull the gown closed about her.

There was a knock, and a woman with a clipboard came in. Calm competence exuded from her. She extended her hand, which Cassie shook. "I'm Dr. Morrow."

"Oh!"

"And is that a good 'Oh' or a bad 'Oh'?"

"I didn't know you were a woman."

Dr. Morrow smiled. "Most women are more comfortable with a woman doctor. Okay?"

She went over Cassie's personal information and took vitals. Cassie tried to relax through the examination, the doctor palpating her stomach several times.

"When was your last period?"

She sat up, wished she could take a shower after such an incursion on her body. "Uhh…November, I guess. I've never been very regular. So can I have the pill?" It blurted out as if the words had a mind of their own.

"The pill?" Astonishment crossed Dr. Morrow's face, and she perched next to Cassie on the table. "My dear girl, you're a bit late for that. I thought you knew?"

"Knew?" The world started to spin and the long drive back to the ranch seemed an insurmountable hurdle. Would she have to call Coop?

"You're about two months pregnant. Didn't you know?"

"I…I guess not. I thought—"

Dr. Morrow's hand rested on Cassie's. "If you were irregular, I imagine it would be hard to tell. No morning sickness then, I take it. But you're most definitely pregnant." She hesitated. "Are you engaged?"

"Oh, lord, no. No, I'm not. I mean…I'm living with someone."

"Will he marry you?"

She jumped up and started to dress in front of the doctor. "No, no, he won't do that. I know he won't."

The doctor extended her hand to turn Cassie to face

her. "There's a case coming up before the Supreme Court to legalize abortion—in just a few days, I understand—"

"Oh, no, no, I couldn't do that. It would be taking a life."

"Then adoption is your only answer if he won't marry you."

Cassie stopped where her hand held a shirt button, looked into the doctor's well-meaning face. "No, Doctor. It isn't the only answer. There is one more. The right one."

****

Coop sat at the kitchen table, beer in hand, the early dark curtaining the windows. Clouds hid the moon, but the wind moved them on, making moments of starlit sky, a moving picture show. For a brief moment, he wondered if she'd taken the truck and headed to California. He wouldn't blame her; what was he offering her here? A love he didn't know how to express, a hard existence on a ranch she knew nothing about, a life away from people she understood. Cassie had never given him any indication she wanted to stay, unless he considered her threats to leave for California such an indication.

The sound of the motor rumbled him out of his reveries, and he stood, flicked the lights on before he stepped out.

"Don't start," she said as she got out of the truck. "I'm back, the journey was fine, the appointment ran late."

"I didn't say a thing. I was worried is all. Come on inside."

She pushed past him into the warmth of the house,

noted nothing had been done toward dinner, and wondered if he'd be able to manage on his own again. She slipped out of her coat and hung it by the door. "I said there was a casserole I'd made, in the fridge. All you had to do was turn on the oven and shove it in."

"Oh, jeez, I forgot. I'm sorry."

His hangdog expression made her soften. "Well, it'll be a while." She turned on the oven to heat, got the dish out, and slid it onto the top shelf in the oven.

"So what did the doctor say, Cass? You get the prescription?"

She considered saying she had it, but he'd soon find out there were no pills around. "Nope."

"No? *No?* Well, why the hell not?"

"Because…she has the right to deny me, that's why." It wasn't a lie, it just wasn't the whole truth.

Coop stared at her, disappointed. "Well, can you see someone else?"

Her mind raced. "I doubt insurance will cover me for endless doctor appointments until I find someone who will give me the pill, Coop. And even if it did, I'm not going to put myself through that examination again."

"Oh."

"Yes, 'oh.' I'm sorry if you don't like…the alternatives."

"What about that thing, that cup or whatever it's called. Women used to use that before the pill came along."

She went to the door, kept her face away from his sight. "I can see about it, I guess. I can go back to her. She didn't mention it. Birth control is birth control. They don't like encouraging premarital sex." She waited for a response but none came. "I have to go shower. Dinner'll be about forty-five minutes."

She climbed the steps, rethinking what had gone through her mind all the way home. She had never really considered having children, even when she thought of marriage to Coop. Back home, friends were already having babies, but her idea had been to set out, have experiences, an adventure, and where had all that gone? Motherhood and marriage had never been her big dream as it was for some little girls; watching *Route 66* on TV had given her a different dream. But then she had met Coop, seen Wyoming, ditched her hippie friends, and stayed—and ended up with a life she had never envisaged. And now that life was coming to an end. She was going to have a baby, would have to look after the child on her own and take responsibilities she knew she couldn't foresee. Maybe that was an adventure, too. One thing she did know: she was going to love the child and care for it, whatever the future brought. Even if it meant leaving Coop.

****

Sometime during the night he made up his mind. He didn't know how he'd come to the idea, whether it was the way they made love that evening, or the good feel of just having her around, safe and sound, but the answer suddenly seemed so simple it surprised him. The only worry was whether Cassie would go along with it all.

"Got errands in town," he mumbled as he pecked her on the cheek. "Be gone the morning. You doing anything special today?"

"I'll go through the seed catalogs again, maybe have a think about that braiding you suggested, and I have some baking to do."

He perched on the side of the bed near her. "Really? You gonna think about the braiding?" He tried to keep the hopefulness out of his voice. It wasn't the braiding itself he wanted her to do, it was the idea of a long-term occupation he liked, the sense she would stay, *wanted* to stay.

There was a small smile on her face, and she reached out and pulled him down for a kiss. "*Think* about the braiding."

Coop laughed. "Okay then, *think*."

Later, he waved to her as she stood at the upstairs window, thought she looked rather sad, but he considered this idea of his should cheer her up. In town, the man at the hardware shop noted Coop's cheerfulness.

"You look like the cat what got the cream today, Mr. Byrnes."

"Yeah, maybe." He flicked through the catalog he was holding. "John, you got any ideas about greenhouses? You know, them really big ones like they got in the garden centers?"

"Well, they cost a bunch and—"

"Oh, I'm not worrying about the cost in particular. I want something good, long-lasting, I can set on my forty nearest the house."

"You know you're gonna need a base. Most are cement blocks, but I know other stuff can be used. And it's all gotta be anchored down, otherwise, first gale we get, your greenhouse could end up being my greenhouse, they're so lightweight."

Coop grimaced. "Sounds complicated. Well, I'll figure something out."

"And you know you gotta put it all together, most of 'em, anyways. Glass and frames and so on. Big job."

He tried not to let his annoyance show. "Since when was a job too big for me, John? I never shirked a job in my life."

"All right, all right, keep your shirt on. Just making sure you know what's ahead. I don't want complaints down the road—I didn't tell you this, I didn't mention that. Just so's you know, is all."

"Well, let me have a look. Maybe I'll get something a mite smaller to start, and if it takes off, we can always get something bigger."

"Good idea." John moved back to another customer at the counter while Coop strummed through his catalog.

There was one greenhouse that kept catching his eye—galvanized steel frame…pre-welded stanchions… It had a commercial-grade eight-millimeter twin-wall corrugated roof and walls six feet tall, with a center peak of nine and a half feet for optimal air circulation…eight feet long. *Yup, that's the one. She'll love that.*

Outside, a slushy snow hit the streets and stayed as an unwanted guest, glistening the pavement in the gray light. He pulled his jacket collar up, thankful for the covering along the boardwalk as he made his way back to his truck. At the corner, as he stood under the shelter waiting for the light to change, he glanced into the shop there.

Jewelry. Rings. *Engagement* rings.

The light changed, and he started across, sleepwalking almost, but he stopped in the middle of the road. A car honked angrily, helping him come to his senses.

What had he been thinking? That a greenhouse, of all things, was what Cassie would want, what would keep her in Wyoming? Was he plumb out of his mind? There was only one thing that would keep Cassie in Wyoming—of that he could be sure.

He turned back.

He'd never been in a jewelry shop, and for a moment he almost pivoted back out again. The lit cases, the glare of the gold and the sparkle of the diamonds, the hush. It was seductive and almost embarrassing at once. When the salesgirl came over and asked if he needed help, he suddenly felt like bolting out the door, uncertain yet mesmerized by the display.

"Are you looking for something in particular? Engagement rings?"

"Yeah," he said, his voice soft. "Engagement rings."

She led him to a far counter and went behind. "Do you know her size? Do you have a budget?"

"What?"

"How much do you want to spend?" There was some amusement in her voice, but enough patience to let him think.

"Oh. I hadn't thought. Well. She's got to like it, is all."

"All right, well, what sort of woman is she? A cowgirl? Or…"

"Oh, no, no, she's…well, she's different. I mean, she's not from hereabouts, and she likes to cook and garden and make things."

The salesgirl bit her lip. "I see. Well." She pulled out a tray. "Prices here start around a thousand dollars.

Are you comfortable with that?" She looked at him bright-eyed, hopeful.

"Oh yeah, sure." His eyes scanned the tray, and he reached for a ring that was fairly simple, a small marquise diamond with two baguettes, set in white gold. He turned it over. "That's nice."

The woman brought out a small velvet pillow and he placed it down on that.

"Anything else strike you?"

"I don't know. Maybe she'd like something a bit fancier. Maybe not." He skimmed over the rows. "What about those down there?" He pointed to another tray under the glass in the case.

"Those are a bit more expensive. Those start at three thousand. Would you like to see them?"

"Three thousand? Yeah, I would."

He caught the raised brow of the woman, and a finger of anger hit him. *What, does she think I'm some penniless yokel or something?* He could see that the stones in these rings were slightly larger, wondered if Cassie would think him a fool for spending so much, buying such a large ring. Would she complain it got in the way of her baking and gardening? She often disparaged waste and had such peculiar opinions; maybe she wasn't going to want a diamond anyway; maybe she'd tell him to take it back.

"Well," he said at last, "I don't really see anything I like better than that one."

"It has lovely clarity and color. No flaws. We can size it to her finger if you like."

"Oh, hell. I have no idea what size her finger is. She's a slender little thing."

"Well, you can always come in later. With her.

Would you like it engraved?"

"Engraved? How? With what?" His gaze searched her face.

"Both your initials. The date of the wedding, maybe. A few simple words?"

"Okay then."

The woman brought over a pad and pen and handed it to Coop, who scribbled down his few words and handed it back.

"Oh," she said looking at what he had written. "We may have to wait until after sizing so the engraving isn't ruined if the size has to be changed. I'll let you know, but we'll try."

"Oh. Okay." He stood for a moment staring down at the ring on the little pillow, thinking of what it represented. He envisaged Cassie's excitement, her throwing her arms around him, her smile, maybe a little dance in the kitchen, a special meal. He couldn't help the smile that suddenly stretched his lips.

"So I'll take that," he said at last. He scratched his phone number on the pad beside the words he'd written for the engraving. "You phone me when it's ready, and if we find it doesn't fit, we'll come back in."

Chapter Eleven

She would keep that image of him in her mind, his glance up as he got in his truck, the little wave, the slouch of his Stetson, and the half-smile as if he were trying to stop himself from feeling anything more than the need to get on with work. She hadn't much experience of being in love—a childhood crush, a guy she had dated for a while in college who had thrown her over. Cooper was a man, and maybe loving a man went deeper, or maybe just being older put you more in touch with your own emotions. But his comments that he didn't want to marry her, that he didn't want any "accidents" replayed through her brain.

She rushed to get him some meals made, put burger patties in the freezer, set a slow casserole on to cook. She changed the sheets on the bed and the towels, trying to leave a fresh feeling as if she had never been, were it not for the cooking. She gathered her things to leave no trace, wondered about the coat, whether it was hers to take, and decided she'd better have it. What good would it do Coop except remind him of the strange girl he'd lived with for the better part of nine months. She wondered if he'd remember her in a few years, whether he'd ever think of her, whether he'd even care she was gone.

In the guest room, she threw the last of her clothes into the bag. Next, she stopped at the room they'd shared, the bed where they'd so often made love. Pen and paper on a side table. A note? Cassie stood with the pen in her hand, nibbling her thumbnail, tried to keep from crying, but it was no use. *Dear Coop, thanks for everything. I love you, Cassie.* It sounded too businesslike. Abrupt. She crumpled it and threw it in the bin. *Coop, I love you but I never meant to be a burden. Think of me kindly sometimes if you can, Cassie.* She checked around one more time to make sure she had all her things, trudged down the stairs, grabbed her new coat off the peg, and headed out.

A watery snow fell and melted as soon as it hit the ground. It suddenly struck her that she had to get out before Coop got back, so she wouldn't have to face his ire. She couldn't deal with that, couldn't go through a goodbye scene. And where was she heading? Down the Teton Pass to Idaho and west? Or might it be easier at Hoback, miles away, to go south first and across?

Hank's truck was there, and in the distance, in the pasture, she could just make him out afoot, the dogs prancing around him, tails wagging, just coming in toward the yard. He stopped when he saw her, called out, his voice lost on the wind. He had been very considerate to her, and she'd miss him, his gentle ways, his kindnesses, but it was best not to stop.

She went on, tried not to look his way, spied him jumping over the far corral fence and heading toward her. She kept going, emptiness opening up in her like a sinkhole.

"Cassie! Cassie, wait!" Breathless, he came up and grabbed her arm. The dogs were yapping as if they sensed something wrong. "Where in tarnation are you going on foot, sweetheart?" He turned her to him.

She stood silent, sniffed, then wiped her nose on the back of her hand before rummaging in her coat pocket for a tissue.

Hank looked down at the satchel in her hand. "Oh, Cassie, no. Whatever he did, Coop didn't mean anything by it, sweetheart. You must know by now he's all roar of the lion, gentle as a lamb. Heck, Cassie."

She stood and faced him, silent for a heartbeat as the dogs circled her. "He didn't do anything," she said at last. "I have to go, that's all. It's time."

"Time for what, for heaven's sake? Oh, Cassie, the man's in love with you. I can see it in his face, even if he never says a word."

"No, no, he's not! I have to go. I don't want to have to say goodbye, and I can make it to somewhere by tonight."

"What somewhere, for heaven's sake? Have you got any money, even? Oh, Cassie, think. The dead of winter and you hitching? What sense is that?"

Cassie grabbed Hank and gave him a quick hug, bent to ruffle each dog, then turned to march away.

It wasn't long before his truck pulled up beside her.

"Get the hell in, if you're set on going. I'll at least take you down to Hoback."

****

It was early afternoon by the time Coop drove in the gate, surprised not to see Hank's truck in the yard. He slammed the door behind him and practically skipped into the house, calling for Cassie, happy and excited about what he was doing. The only reply came from Wayne and Elam, who gathered around him before he pushed them aside and closed them in the gunroom. The smell of some stew she had set in the crockpot hit him, and he was tempted to lift the lid and see what it was, but he knew he'd get his hand slapped. It made him smile to think he knew her ways so well.

"Cass?" His voice seemed to echo back in the quiet, and he glanced outside once more to see if she were there. Maybe she had saddled her gelding and gone for a ride, but he doubted that, in this weather.

"Cass?" He called again as he mounted the steps, took them two at a time, looked in the guest room, saw the bathroom door open and the towels changed. He opened the door to the bedroom and found everything tidy just as Hank's truck sounded in the yard. That would be it. Maybe she had some errand, and Hank had taken her.

Coop stood at the window and looked down into the yard as Hank seemed to move in slow motion out of his truck, crippled-like, and pushed the door shut behind him. He spotted Cooper's truck and looked up at the window, their gazes meeting for a brief moment before Hank turned away and came toward the house.

An icicle of fear slipped down Coop's back, chalk on a blackboard, and he shivered, flipped his hat on the bed, moved toward the door, and spotted the note on the table. White like snow. Folded. "Coop" written in Cassie's childish but bold hand. He stared at it, saw the other crinkled paper in the waste basket and took it out, smoothing it like a sheet for a bed. *Dear Coop, thanks for everything, I love you.* A bruise in his chest started, a mild pain that would deepen and grow like a cancer. He heard Hank mount the steps at last, saw him lean into the doorframe, stare at him with a gray look, haggard.

"She leave you a note?" Hank's voice was tired,

flat.

He handed over the one from the trash bin and waited as Hank read it, passed it back.

"I tried to convince her, said you really loved her and wouldn't want her going, but she'd just got it in her head you wanted her out."

"Out?" His head felt foggy, and he couldn't focus.

"I don't know, Coop. I got years on you and still can't figure women, where they get their dang ideas."

"Where is she now? Where'd she go? Dang woman'll freeze to death." He held the folded note in his hand, slightly out as if to bring it too close would cause more pain.

"She was gonna walk, Lord knows where, and there was no use arguing. I took her down to Hoback Junction, parked on the shoulder, and watched until she got a ride."

"A ride! What, with some murderer, for all you know? Hank, for chrissake!"

Hank sighed, shook his head. "Coop, I tried to convince her to stay. It was like talking to a brick wall, and I figured the best I could do was make sure she got a ride somewhere, wherever she was headed. If she'd walked, she'd be froze to death within the hour."

He felt like he was suffocating, his breath gone out of his lungs, dizzy for a moment. The note was still in his hand, unopened, and he brought it in now and slowly unfolded it.

Coop, I love you but I never meant to be a burden. Think of me kindly sometimes if you can, Cassie.

"A burden?" He breathed out the word. "A burden? When were you ever a burden, damn you! When did I ever say you were a burden!" He clutched the note in his hand, crumpled it.

"You come on now to Maggy and me for dinner, stay the night, think 'bout what you want to do—"

"No. No, I'll be fine." He collapsed on the bed and shook his head, thoughts flying through his mind as leaves one might try to grab in the wind. "Why?" he said to himself. "Why would she do this? I just…"

Hank's face showed a mask of uncertainty, pain. "Coop?"

"You best go on. Maggy will be waiting, Hank. You go on home now."

"You're not gonna do anything foolish now, are you?"

He looked up and snorted. "Me? When did I ever do anything 'foolish'? Aside, of course, from bringing a dang hippie home and letting her live here for nine months." His laugh was bitter, hollow. He took a last look at the note she'd written and tossed it in the trash.

"Okay, then."

He sat and listened to Hank's steps as he descended the stairs and shut the door behind him. When he'd heard the truck start up, spin on the ice for a moment, and leave, he ran a hand through his hair, took a last glance in wonder at the way she had left the room—so tidy, spotless—and headed down to the kitchen.

The crockpot was bubbling away now, and he unplugged it, stared at it a moment, then lifted the entire pot and flung it at the wall. He stood and stared as the brown mess slid, like a lava flow, down onto the floor below.

Then he collapsed at the table and for the first time in nearly thirty years cried like a baby.

Part Two: Chapter Twelve

July 1973

Unspoken Feelings are Unforgettable.
                              ~Andrei Tchaikovsky

She kept going, through every pain, every contraction, sorry she had opted for natural childbirth and then, when she held the baby, glad she had done it that way. An ecstasy—deep overwhelming happiness—came to her, holding the child in her arms, as she felt it suckle. Someone who was hers, who would love her.

One social worker had hammered on to give the baby up for adoption, but Cassie steadfastly refused, lied that the father was coming to marry her soon and, until then, she could manage on her own. Then another social worker appeared. Uncalled for, unwanted, yet demanding. The doctors had reported Cassie and called the woman in.

"I have the papers here. I don't know why they let you see her and hold her. It's not the done thing. It makes you attached—"

Groggy, she sat up. She eyed the baby, safe in the basinet to her side, curtains drawn between herself and the other mothers with whom she shared the room. She could feel their ears growing, listening, holding their breaths to see what would transpire, disgusted at her.

"I am attached." Cassie's voice was low. "I'm twenty-three, nearly twenty-four, I have a right—"

"Come, now, we're not talking about rights, your rights, we're talking about what is best for the baby here—"

"The baby has a name. Her name is Jacky, short for Jackson."

"Well, of course, my dear, you may call her whatever you wish. The adoptive parents will want to name her themselves."

"There'll be no adoptive parents!" Cassie raised her voice. She no longer cared who heard. She wiggled in the bed to sit up better, as much as the movement hurt her underneath. The discomfort was nothing compared to her fight for her child.

"You have to move on, forget. You want your baby to have the best life possible, don't you? Won't a married couple be so much better than an emotionally immature young girl who didn't know any better than to waste her virtue before marriage? You hippies are all the same."

Desperation was overcoming her now. "I did not waste my virtue! My virtue was having Jacky, was loving a man who loved me—"

"Loved you enough to marry you?" When Cassie didn't respond, she continued, "You want your daughter to start life as an illegitimate child, doomed to failure? Is that what you want for her?" She took a few steps closer to the bed.

Jacky started to fuss, her little cries a prelude to something louder.

Cassie struggled out of her bed and lifted her child into her arms, protective, unyielding.

"You'll be able to return to your old life, whatever that may be. And your child will be given a new life—with two parents. Isn't that what you really want for her? The best for you both?"

She looked down at her baby as her child gurgled and smiled up at her. "No. Absolutely not. I will not be parted from her, and you can't make me."

"And where do you live? This address I've been given—over in the Haight, with the hippies and dropouts. You refuse to sign the papers, Child Welfare will be checking on you. Every day. You'll see. You'll see how long you want to keep her."

****

The other members of the commune resented the constant intrusion of the child welfare officer, showing up unannounced. They feared they'd get in trouble, with their bongs and roaches left lying about, the smell of pot heavy in the air. And Cassie, who feared the effect of all that smoke on her baby, had looked for another place to stay to no avail. The welfare officer advised her to try to get out, would have started proceedings yet held back, seemed to understand her predicament and love for her baby. The baby was happy enough, even thriving; the officer ignored the others in the house on the grounds Cassie had her own room and noted it, apparently, as a separate apartment.

San Francisco was expensive. The jobs she'd had were unrewarding, and the memory of Coop's ranch remained always in the back of her mind. She missed the warmth, the routine, the surety of his being there, and she daydreamed about returning, about what he'd say when he saw their little girl, and if he'd soften and marry her. It was a fantasy, as she envisaged the knock on the door one day—he'd managed to track her, find her, and would take her home. But that didn't happen, and she had to accept Coop was never coming for her as she had imagined. A dream. Nothing but a dream.

She was pleased she'd had a little girl. A boy might have reminded her too often of Coop and made her wonder if the boy should have his father growing up. But a girl she could handle. And the others in the house loved the baby, too, even if they moaned about the social worker. They played with the little girl, helped Cassie, bought things from the thrift shops, shared babysitting so she could work at the café.

"Your shirt is wet, sweetie. You got a problem?" The owner wiped his hands on a dishtowel, something between a snarl and a sneer on his face. "Look, I know you want this job, but I can't have you dripping on the diners."

"No, no, I'll get the pump and—"

"Pump it out?" He scowled. "What do you do with it then?"

"Put it in the fridge and take it home for the next day."

"You been doing this before?"

"Yes."

There was a long pause. "Whatcha bottle look like?"

"I sterilize a small milk bottle." Worry grew in her as to where this was leading.

"I see." There was another long pause as the boss played with the dishtowel in his hands. "You didn't notice you was missin' a bottle one day?"

"I thought someone had thrown it out by mistake."

"Mistake, huh? Look, I served that damn stuff to

someone here for their coffee—they complained our milk was off." He let this sink in, scrutinized her reaction, or lack of one. "I'm sorry, Cassie, you're gonna have to go. Go and come back when you stop leaking like that, will ya. You're a damn good worker, and I like you, but I can't have this here."

She stared at the man, disbelief mixing with wonder at what she could do next.

"I'll get your wages for ya."

The early autumn heat rose from the sidewalks, wavered the views out to the bay like a watercolor painting. People sat on their front stoops in The Haight, fanned themselves with newspapers, watched kids playing in the streets, or made deals on the street corners, in the open. She loved the ornate houses here with their balconies, bay windows, and gingerbread work, the way they promenaded up the hill and down the hill like soldiers in line. She thought being near the Golden Gate Park was a bonus, somewhere Jacky could play when she grew, somewhere to take her in the sling she had fashioned, yet it troubled her to be in the midst of so much drug traffic.

When she trudged up the steps to the commune house earlier than usual, she stood outside on the porch; an open window let out strains of Jefferson Airplane mixed with conversation from the living area.

"Listen, man, I can't sleep at night with that baby wailing. I like the kid, I really do, but it's, like, really toying with my psyche."

"I know what you mean," came another voice. "It's really cool to have a baby in the house but just not practical. Look at how much time we have to spend caring for her. Cute as she is."

"Yeah I vote against, too. Cassie's just not adding a lot to the community here, always having to care for the kid. I'm sorry, but that's the way I feel."

She pulled the screen door open, glanced into the living room, the baby gurgling and dribbling in the center of a circle of stoned hippies who solemnly discussed her as they passed a joint. The group went quiet at her entry. Some heads turned her way; others bowed and avoided her.

"Hey, Cassie," the appointed leader said. "Home early."

She went over and picked up Jacky, rubbed her nose against the warm skin. "It's okay. I'll leave as soon as I can find someplace else, all right?"

"That's it, actually," the leader said. "We know a couple of guys up in Bolinas, gays, who say they'd be happy to have you there. And Jacky, too, of course. You just have to keep house for them, cook and clean, like, but you get a room and food, and they'll let Jacky stay. It'll be cool for you, living and working on the spot, no need for help with Jacks here, and it's really groovy up in Bolinas."

She lifted her baby up in the air, cooing happily, a game, a joy, and brought her back to her shoulder. "That's great. Just great. Where the hell is Bolinas?"

****

Dave drove her up to Bolinas in a truck he borrowed from work, the baby in her arms, the stuff she had accumulated in the bed of the truck. She wondered if she had grown up, matured ahead of the others, because of Coop or because of the responsibility of Jacky. She felt detached from them all, since she'd denied herself the joints and LSD first because of her pregnancy, then because of the responsibility now laid on her shoulders. She was glad to be out, to be away from that atmosphere, out in the country again. It wasn't Wyoming, but as they drove in silence up Route 101, she felt a sense of new beginnings, an adventure. Or going home.

The road they took into town was unmade, nothing more than an old mule track, perhaps, leading down to Bolinas and the bay it spilt onto. Houses were scattered like thrown dice, sitting where they fell, until they got to the one main street, or what passed for it, leading down to the shore. Cassie loved it already, an excitement mounting, and Jacky must have felt it, too, for she giggled and bounced in her mother's arms.

"I'm sorry about the group decision. It wasn't mine," Dave muttered.

"It's fine. This is better. I prefer being out in the country anyway. It's better for Jacky."

"I would've married you. Still would." He turned to see her reaction, but she only had eyes for the baby now and ignored his remark. "You still in love with that piece of shit from Wyoming?"

She turned sharply. "He wasn't a piece of shit. It was my decision. He didn't know." She wondered if that were the truth, if Coop might have married her had he known but "we don't want any accidents" played again through her mind.

She jostled the baby on her lap for a moment, then asked, "So how did you guys find out about these men?"

"Howie met them in a gay bar, or maybe knew them, not sure. He told them about the commune, and they asked if he knew anyone suitable. They're old.

Well, elderly, I take it. Like in their fifties or something. But they're cool."

"In what way?"

"Oh, you know, they'll let you smoke pot and stuff, they don't care, as long as you do your job. I think one of them, Larry, maybe—their names are Larry and Gary by the way, so don't laugh when you're introduced— has a ton of money from somewhere or other."

Cassie bit her lip, her sense of anticipation giving way to some humor about where she had ended up.

They pulled in at a rambling home that had the countenance of having been a tree house that dropped to earth and subsequently had bits added to anchor it to the ground, all weathered wood and cross-paned windows, a skirted roof circling each of two halves connected by a covered dogtrot. She felt like Alice about to fall through the looking glass, or Dorothy landing in Oz. A damp breeze blew in off the sea, and she could taste the salt on her lips. Holding Jacky closer, she wondered whether the child was warm enough.

After parking, they marched up a flagstone path. Dave carried her things while she held the baby, and they came to a door painted pink. Dave plunked her gear at her feet and rang the bell. There was the sound of shuffling footsteps; slippers flapped on a wood floor.

"Oh, my dear," said a man with a face like putty as he pulled open the door. "We're *sooo* very happy to have you. And the child, of course. Come in, come in."

"I'll go now," Dave intruded. "It's an hour back, and I promised to get the truck in before five."

"Oh." She pivoted to him, torn between losing this lifeline that was about to exit yet wanting rid of him.

"It's fine."

"Well, what a pity you couldn't stay for tea. Larry's baked for the occasion." He turned to her. "I'm Gary, by the way. I know it gets confusing to some— Larry and Gary. Anyway, my dear, do come in." He seemed uninterested in Dave's departure and flipped his hand in a farewell gesture as Dave waited for her to say something.

"Bye," was all she said, relieved of his closeness, the reminder of that night in the dance hall, the yearning in his eyes, always the insistence he wanted her.

Gary stepped out onto the paving stones and lifted her two bags as Dave first stood back, then turned and left. As she followed Gary into the hall, she heard the rumble of the truck and its struggle up the hill and out of Bolinas.

"I didn't think anyone here cooked or baked. I understood that was what you wanted me for."

"Oh, my dear, but we do. Larry has got *so* lazy in his dotage, but he apparently thought we should have a little special welcome. And so we should, and so we should!"

He led the way into their kitchen, where the other man stood, towering over the counter. A mop of gray hair fell about a grizzled face, yet he wore a woman's apron and slippers.

"*Darling*," Gary drawled, "Look who's come. And with the sweet baby as well. We're a family at last, dear heart—we have a wife!"

****

Her room, with the baby, was a large space in the upper story, along with its own bathroom, away from the men, whose rooms were on the other side of the dogtrot. It peered out onto Bolinas Bay, was sunny and bright, and bigger than any she'd ever had. The heating came up, but she was reluctant to admit she needed it, although the all-pervasive damp air of the Pacific coast inhabited her bones. Jacky happily chirped away as she crawled around the great floor and basked in the trapezoid of sunlight that had made its way in.

During the day, she carried Jacky in the sling, was happy to push the vacuum around and cook their meals.

Coop was always at the back of her mind, an ache, a paper cut that bothered her when her mind was left alone. The baby took most of the pain away, though the child served as both a reminder and a panacea. As Cassie settled into a routine, feeling welcomed by the gay couple and coming to love their humor and their humanity, she felt more at home. It struck her they were an odd couple, and not because they were men. Gary with his podgy, ebullient ways, his theatricality, served as a foil to Larry, tall and patrician, quiet and reserved, although he could be a drama queen as well, at times.

"I am not a crook!" Larry stood, one hand out, trying to imitate President Nixon. "But I do want a spectacular Thanksgiving dinner, please, dear heart. I can help, of course."

She tried not to laugh, then gave in to the fun. "And so you shall have it."

She prepared them roast Brussels sprouts and turkey, potatoes duchesse, and a Waldorf salad, string beans almondine, and both pecan pie and pumpkin pie, the latter flooding her with memories at every bite. Jacky was passed between them all, happy drops of spittle needing to be wiped by their fine linen napkins in the candlelight.

They drank wine from crystal goblets, which gave her the temerity to ask, "Didn't you want any friends to come tonight? There's plenty of food."

"Oh no, my dear." Gary exchanged glances with his lover. "It's far too far to come down from the city on Thanksgiving Day, and anyway, we wanted you all to ourselves."

She looked from one to the other. Tweedle Dum and Tweedle Dee. She laughed, and Jacky laughed too. And then the men laughed at the baby, so they were all giggling in their own way, not even knowing why they were so happy.

****

"We're going to the city," Gary announced one day. "What would you like? We're buying Christmas presents and anything else you need, dear one. Just say the word."

Cassie stomped on the pedal of the vacuum, made a slight turn to check Jacky, who was crawling around, and faced Gary. "Good olive oil would be nice."

"Good…?" His mouth dropped open. "Oh, no, no, you misunderstand. I meant for Christmas, something extravagant, a mink coat or a diamond ring…"

She stood, hand on hip to show her disapproval, her cheeks blown out in a smirk.

"Well, maybe not, then. Olive oil it is."

She spent the afternoon trying to think of what she could do for this couple who were so generous to her and Jacky, and the braiding came back to mind. But not a hatband this time. Perhaps belts, and perhaps she could make something else to go with them. And then she wondered whether Coop still wore the band she'd made for him.

Coop.

Alone in the house with the phone. Would they be able to see she'd made a call to Wyoming? The bill would show it, surely. And what would it accomplish, hearing his voice? Or Mrs. Craven might answer, and then what?

She bashed the pedal of the vacuum, and Jacky started crying, great wails that the noisy monster again interrupted her contented investigation of the room. Cassie put her back in the sling on her hip and finished the carpets. The phone by the bed sat there, its dial like a happy face against the squat pink of the unit, the receiver sitting on top with its coil of plastic cord. Maybe just to hear his voice? But why?

What was there to gain?

Chapter Thirteen

When Dusty and Hank found Coop drunk for the sixth day in a row, they dragged him out to the corral and threw him into the horse trough.

"No quicker way to sober up." Dusty stood and stared as Coop shook his head. Water droplets scattered as he struggled to get out.

"You son of a bitch!" His slurred words faded inside his head at the same time bile rose and he spat.

The men just stood looking on, nodding.

"Damn it! Damn you fucking bastards!"

Hank moved forward, hand extended to help him out. He slid, unable to focus on the hand long enough to grab it, until finally Dusty came around and got him under the arms and pulled him up.

Coop sniffed and ran his hand under his nose; tears mixed with the water from the trough. They held on to him until he stumbled out.

"I'll go make you some coffee," Dusty told him as Coop staggered toward the house.

Inside, Hank settled him in a chair, brought some towels from the bathroom, and stood as Coop ruffled the towel in his face, his hair. Water from his clothes pooled on the floor. Shivering, he pulled the towel around his neck. Then, as Dusty set the mug of coffee in front of him, he grasped it with both hands.

"Son, you're gonna have to sober up and go after

her—or forget her." Dusty leaned back against the counter and gave him a long look. "You can't go on like this. All this work your family put into this ranch, all the things your daddy did to keep this ranch going, you just can't leave it be. And you know that. I know you know that."

Coop sniffed and looked away. The pain of loss burned his insides, a great emptiness, a cavern opened up. Why hadn't he gone after her that day she left? Hank said she'd got a lift, was that it? Too much to do, too much effort to search, too far? Or had he felt she wanted out and so he let her go? He couldn't recall anything but the pain of loss, the ache of desertion, of being cast aside. *Thanks for everything. I didn't want to be a burden.*

Hank pulled out the chair opposite him and sat. His gaze met Dusty's, and the other man headed out the door to his chores.

"You know what you're doing is just plain dumb, Cooper. All your dang life this ranch has been everything to you. What's different now? I admit Cassie was about the sweetest little thing you could hope for, but if it didn't work out between you, you just have to accept that. Get on with your life now."

"I bought her a ring. I was going to ask her to marry me."

Hank's face scrunched with the sting of that knowledge. "Did she know?" His words came out slowly, like movement with pain.

"No." He sounded hoarse. He rocked in his chair, tried to get the mug to his mouth.

Hank sat back. "Jesus, Coop. That girl thought you didn't love her."

The coffee slopped over the edge of the mug as he set it on the table, then tried to pick it up again. He looped a finger through the handle and clasped it with his other hand, shaking, to get a sip and swallow. The hot liquid warmed his insides. "I don't know how she couldn't know. I was living with her. What in tarnation did she think was going on here? I was caring for her, or at least I thought I was. Sleeping with her, loving her. What did she think that was? A game? Playing house?"

Hank's hand scrubbed across his chin. "You ever tell her? Say the words?"

"No, 'course not. What the hell good are words? Empty, meaningless. Didn't I show her every day I loved her?"

Hank sat back and sighed. "Well, Coop, I don't know what to say, 'cept a woman likes to hear that stuff and know for sure a man loves her—have him verify it, I guess, by saying it."

"Well, I never heard my father say it to my mother." He took another gulp of the black liquid, staring into the cup.

"And how did that work out, then?"

Coop barked out a laugh before the two men sat staring at each other.

Outside, a gray day was beginning to announce more snow ahead.

"I better change, I guess." He rose unsteadily and downed the coffee. "I'm sorry for what you and Dusty had to put up with these last few days. Sorry to have done this to you. I'll try to see it doesn't happen again."

****

He turned it all over in his mind once more.

Perhaps if he had gone down the road with some sort of description from Hank of the car she had got into, would he have found her? Got them to pull over? Dragged her home? Haight-Ashbury, San Francisco, wasn't much to work on, he knew. The likelihood of finding her there not great. Did she even make it there, or did she get waylaid as she had here? It made no sense to try to find her, a waste of time, and would put too many responsibilities on Dusty and Hank's shoulders. Still, his heart hungered for her. He felt the emptiness in bed each night, the cold spot where once there had been warmth, the vacancy of the kitchen when he went down in the morning and got his own breakfast, ate his meals on his own, heard the forlorn whine of the dogs, who still seemed to search for her.

Yet he got the drinking under control, got to bed early, three drinks only, and with an iron will pulled himself upstairs to the void of the bedroom. In silence, he went through the bedtime routine, and tried to forget Cassie wasn't there, while not reflecting on where she might be, where she might have gone.

The phone rang one lunchtime when he had come in. A can of dog food in his hand, he cut his finger slightly on the open lid as he picked up the handset.

"Hello?" He licked the spot of blood appearing on his finger and put the can down.

"Mr. Byrnes? This is the jewelry shop in town. You remember?"

He stood frozen to the spot, the receiver in his hand by his ear, but he said nothing.

"Mr. Byrnes, are you there?"

"Yes. I'm here."

"We have your ring, sir. We've called several

times for you to collect it."

"You have." His reply came automatically, dumbly.

The woman hesitated. "We can't take it back because it's engraved now, I'm afraid." More upbeat, she added, "We were able to do your engraving and still leave a spot where it might be either enlarged or taken in."

"I see."

The hesitation in the woman's voice showed her disquiet. "Can you come in and collect it? Please. We can't be responsible for it any longer."

"I see." He looked down at Elam, who barked and tried to jump onto the counter, paws clawing toward his food. "I'll come and get it. She'll love it."

Somewhere in his mind, he still saw himself giving it to her, getting down on one knee, even—they liked that, women, he told himself. But the knowledge she would never see it haunted him, tormented him. In the shop, he made the transaction as swiftly as possible. When the woman offered to show it to him before she wrapped it, he declined.

"I trust you. It's fine," he said.

He sensed the woman seemed to know not to push the point, not to say he'd best check that the inscription was correct, that it was the right ring.

That night, he sat dinnerless with his beer at the table, held the ring to the light, turned it over in his hands, noted the engraving, and wondered how they did that, how they got those words on the inside of the band. He could see where the space had been left should the size need adjusting, and marveled at how they had figured that out. Cassie would love it.

Would've loved it, he corrected himself as he tossed it back onto the kitchen table.

****

He was out in the north pasture forking down hay bales from the back of a flat bed while Dusty drove when the roar of a big rig came by on his ranch road. He jumped down and went to Dusty's window.

"Well, what the heck is that?" Dusty sat watching as the truck maneuvered several times to turn into the gate.

"Damned if I know." He leaned an elbow on Dusty's open window, head in hand. And then it struck him. He knew exactly what was being delivered. "Oh, shit, I better get back." He jumped in the truck and slammed the door.

"Strange thing, a rig that big coming in. Must be lost."

"No, he ain't lost." His voice held a note of disgust. "I just completely forgot."

Dusty parked a distance away so the truck could turn back out when it left. Coop jumped down.

"I don't want that thing," he shouted before he was even up close to the man who knocked on the door. "You can take that back."

The man turned, disbelief on his face. "Mister, I can't take it back now. It's not returnable. These things are made to order, and anyway, you'd have to sort that with the shop where you ordered it." He held out a clipboard. "Sign here, please."

"What if I don't sign?"

The man huffed out his disbelief and shook his head. "Then I just dump it down here anyway and write 'no one at home to receive.' You don't want it, you

153

should have canceled the dang order."

Coop stood, hands on hips, looking at the ground and considered. Somewhere in the back of his mind, he believed Cassie was going to return—she'd just stroll up the road one day and ask to come back—and how overjoyed she'd be when she saw the greenhouse. "Okay then." He took the clipboard and scrawled his signature. "You can offload it over there."

"You got a base for it yet?"

"No."

The man glanced at him as if he were dealing with a crazy person. "That's pretty muddy," he noted.

"Just put the damn thing over there, and I'll deal with it!"

For days, he walked past the piles of bits and pieces wrapped in plastic and cardboard, an instruction booklet poking out from one packet with the plates of glass. More and more, as the weather warmed into spring, the idea grew on him that Cassie would return and everything would be fine, he should proceed with building it. Finally, instead of eating lunch, he spent his breaks assembling what he needed—spirit level, wrenches, posthole digger, cement and gravel, pliers and tape measure. And he started the job, driving the backhoe to clear ground for the base.

As the evenings grew lighter, he spent more time on the greenhouse, a stickler for getting everything right. He measured for the embedment fittings, mixed and poured concrete for the base, dug the holes for the pipes, and filled the pipes with sand to keep the greenhouse weighted down. He kneeled to inspect that everything would be level so the glass would fit perfectly, found it wanting, ripped it out, and started again.

"You'll be driving yourself crazy," Hank said, coming by one evening to help.

"She'll like this," he mumbled, half to himself.

Hank stopped and looked at him, Coop catching his gaze out of the corner of his eye. "And if she doesn't come back?" Hank asked in a slow drawl.

"She will, she will." He glanced up and smiled. "You can count on it. Where else would she go?"

The framing went quickly. He assembled the gables and the sides, mounted the roof and roof vents, constructed the door.

Hank helped when he could.

Coop realized Hank believed he had got some quixotic idea in his head that Cassie would return one day and start planting again, use the greenhouse, wear the ring that sat on his kitchen table, which no one dared touch and no one dared mention. Even Mrs. Craven kept her mouth shut about it all, but he noted she and Hank or Dusty occasionally exchanged glances as they passed. One evening Mrs. Craven stayed on when he had started to clean down the frames with acetone prior to putting in the glass. When he finished, he got the silicone gun in his hand.

"What are you looking at?" He glanced up at the robust housekeeper, her hands on her hips, thumbs hooked in the tie of her dirty apron.

"I'm watching you waste as much time as possible on something that'll never be used."

He pivoted to her, a feeling of betrayal and bewilderment stealing his concentration. "What the hell do you mean? 'Course it'll be used."

She looked at him, shook her head, and started

back to the house. "If you say so," she called over her shoulder.

One evening in June, as they all watched him clip the last piece of glass into the greenhouse, Dusty whispered to Hank, "Cooper's Taj Mahal."

"I heard that," he said. "Well. You think what you damn well want to think." He stood back and admired his handiwork. "Bet that's about the best dang greenhouse anyone's ever built hereabouts."

"Yeah. That's because no one in Wyoming is dumb enough to try to build a greenhouse on a ranch." Dusty laughed.

Hank shook his head at the older man. "You're just jealous, is what it is. You wish you had built something so fine as that."

"Like hell."

But Coop ignored them both. The picture in his mind's eye of Cassie trudging up the road, her satchel in her hand, the coat he'd given her over her arm, was clear in his mind's eye, real. In September, he watched the Battle of the Sexes Tennis Match knowing how Cassie would be rooting for Billy Jean King. He sat through some of the Watergate hearings, her voice in his head, glad Nixon was on his way out. By the time Vice President Spiro Agnew resigned on October tenth, his picture of her return, coming back up the road, had her wearing the coat, a woolen cap pulled down over her ears.

****

One November evening, the need to be with people hit him—not hunger for food but hunger for company, society. He grabbed his coat and his hat, a dark wet night glimmering as he got into the truck. At the dancehall, the lot was crowded with the usual haphazardly parked vehicles, some of which he recognized. As he swung through the doors, he automatically glanced around for familiar faces. Marianne. Ben. Sheila. Even Ty.

"Whiskey," he said to the bartender. "Jack, please."

As the man nodded and turned to get the bottle, then poured a finger into a glass, Coop saw Marianne across the room. And Ty. He slugged the drink back when it came, never taking his eyes off his former girlfriend, then wheeled back to the bar and asked for a second.

"Well, what the hell have we got here?" Ty slapped him on the back, and the drink slopped over the rim of the glass, ran down his fingers. The sweet scent of whiskey rose.

"You're as big an asshole as you ever was, Ty. Go back to whatever cave you crawled outta."

"Well, I thought we could be friends again now." Ty leaned on the bar, his face up close to Coop's. "Seeing as how your girlfriend left you, proving I was right."

"And how's that?"

"Well. She'd of been a decent woman, you'd of married her, wouldn't you? She wouldn't be running off like that, like some two-bit whore."

He knew Ty was trying to wind him up; he had to keep his temper under control. "Maybe I was a jackass, letting her go. What do you know about it anyway?" He shot the Jack back, felt it burn its way down his throat, and called the bartender over for another.

"Well, maybe you are. Maybe that's what you are, Coop, just one giant jackass."

"What's that?" Marianne was suddenly there, her hand resting on Coop's shoulder. "Ty, leave him alone, for chrissake. Go off and find someone else to torment, will ya?"

Ty snorted and started away. "You mind, Marianne, you mind this man. Even he admits he's a jackass."

Marianne shook her head. She settled on a barstool next to Coop and looked at him sympathetically. "I heard that hippie woman left you."

He gripped the edge of the bar and glanced at her sideways. "Well. I guess I deserved it."

"Well. Maybe you did. I don't know. Wanna tell me what happened?"

"Not particularly. Anyway, if I knew myself what happened, maybe I could have fixed it."

Marianne gave a dry laugh. "Well, maybe you could. And maybe you couldn't." She signaled to the bartender for a beer. "All that time we were together, Coop, you treated me like some business proposition. You took me out to dinner, or to a film, then you expected to get laid. If you treated that young gal that way, I can tell you why she left. I can tell you what she felt."

He leaned on the bar and rolled his glass between his hands. *The truth at last?*

Someone had fed the jukebox what seemed endless quarters to play every Johnny Cash song there was. "Ring of Fire" was on now, and he remembered the night he'd met Cassie. Was that it? Had he fallen into that ring of fire? He thought that's how it worked, that you loved someone and they loved you back; you did something for them, and they gave something back. It was actions, not words. Wasn't it?

He looked up at Marianne, the soft blue eyes, full lips. "Sorry, Marianne. I didn't mean to hurt you," he murmured as he stood and tapped his glass down on the bar.

"Are you all right to drive, Coop? Maybe I ought to run you home. Ty can come get me."

"No, I'll be all right. I'll be fine." Suddenly he didn't want the company. He wanted to be alone with his memories of Cassie.

He drove slowly, the windshield wipers sweeping off an icy rain that soon stopped and left the roads glowing as the sky cleared. As he turned onto the ranch road, he could see in the distance the greenhouse now catching the full moon, shimmering, eerie in the bright light. His Taj Mahal, Dusty had called it. He pulled up in front of the house and sat staring, something like dread overcoming him, a deep fear, his blood running cold. Loneliness. Isolation. Decided, he twisted out of the truck and tripped slightly as he made his way to the barn.

He opened the door to the tool shed section, gaped at the implements, some of which he'd employed to get the greenhouse built, and started to pull things off their hooks—wrenches, pliers, then the shovel.

The greenhouse stood before him like some megalith he had to overcome, a monument to his stupidity, to his foolhardiness, his failure. As he threw the pliers, he knew they would do nothing, so the wrenches followed, glass breaking and sliding down in cracked sheets like falling stars. When the wrenches were gone, he at last took the shovel by the neck near the scoop and used it like a baseball bat, hammering at the glass, shattering it into a million pieces that splintered and flew at him and fell to earth like dead birds. But it was his own voice that cried out again and again.

You. Dumb. Bastard. You. Dumb. Bastard.

Chapter Fourteen

1974

It had been Larry's idea that she offer the bake shop her pies, the owners not being bothered about regulations or what her kitchen was like. Gary said she was welcome to use the house kitchen. "It doesn't matter a farthing," he stated in his expansive way, though she had absolutely no idea what a farthing was or what it meant. The shop was excited about her offer and advised she should give her baked goods a name, but all she could come up with was "Cassie's Pies." They had also suggested some brownies with Mary Jane in them, or perhaps a sprinkling of it in a pie, but she declined that notion. After months of denying herself weed while pregnant, she felt the responsibility of motherhood precluded using it at all.

"No matter," the owner had said, "people always find a way."

She had the time, with Jacky strapped to her or left crawling in a corner she deemed safe. The baby's blue eyes were slowly changing, and Cassie could see that the brown/black of Coop's eyes—what he had once called Bay Brown after horse colors—was slowly making an appearance. Sometimes she looked at her child and thought she saw Cooper there, the dimples becoming the brackets around his mouth, somehow the baby's face morphing into his. Their child, she knew, would be a constant reminder of what had been. What could have been. What she still yearned for.

"Oh, my dear, you work *so* hard," Gary said, making a sudden appearance in the kitchen. "Such industriousness. Such care."

"I enjoy keeping busy. I love baking, and gardening, and don't much mind the cleaning, and I love to cook."

"Gardening?" He thought a moment. "Well, for heaven's sake, do something out there! Take as much land as you want—let us have Jacky's beanstalk, straight up to heaven."

"I don't know where your land ends and the neighbors' begins, and I'm not sure what will grow here. The soil's a bit sandy and the salt air breezes are probably not too great for growing stuff." She bent to Jacky and hefted her until Gary took the child to him.

"There's a sweet baby; there's a lamb." He looked back at Cassie. "No one minds, really, where their boundaries are. Just use whatever land you wish, and if it turns out to be someone else's, we'll share the goodies with them. That's my advice. Anyway, our neighbors are *ever* so nice and won't say a word. I promise. You'll discover what grows, I'm sure." He handed Jacky back to her and sauntered off.

She needed seeds and gardening tools, gloves, a hat, and they bought it all for her. Memories of that day in the Jackson hardware shop when Coop had bought her the seeds at the last minute, along with the pressure cooker, flooded through her. His consideration of the black man who'd been waiting, and later the fencing he'd put up around her plot—much against his better judgment. Larry and Gary were good to her, but hadn't Coop been, as well?

Deciding where to start proved difficult, the dry, rocky, sandy soil not particularly inviting for most vegetables, but she managed to get in topsoil, hoe away the rocks, and got "dug in" to a piece of their land on high ground, back from the road a bit. With Jacky on her back, she swizzled in bean poles and got the seeds sown.

"You look like a Chinese coolie," said a voice down on the road.

Azure eyes, like the water you see in Caribbean commercials, stared up at her. A shag of blond hair. A bright white smile.

"What do Chinese coolies look like, then? And anyway, I don't think that's very nice."

"You know, they wear those pointed hats, and the women carry their babies on their backs. *The Good Earth*?"

She tested the pole she had dug in, to make sure it was steady. "Well, I'm not Chinese, for what it's worth."

"I can see that. Who are you?"

She gazed down at him, the slight pinch of his face as he wondered about something—her, perhaps. "I'm Cassie." She slid down the slope toward him. "I work for Larry and Gary." She extended her hand to him.

He looked at it, amusement on his face, then he shook it once. "Dec."

"Deck? I don't understand."

"My name, silly woman. Dec. For Declan. What's Cassie for?"

"Cassie."

"*Okay.* And who's that? On your back?"

Cassie turned around so Jacky could see the man, then pirouetted back. "That's Jacky."

"Like Gleason?"

"*No.* Like Jackson."

"Hmmm. I see. Mississippi? Or after the Cash song?"

"Neither." The baby started crying, and she pulled her around to release her from the sling into her arms. "Wyoming."

"Wyoming. Wow. I bet that's even less populated than Bolinas." He laughed a bit at his joke.

She didn't say anything but lifted Jacky into the air as if she were flying. Jacky laughed, then spit up, dribbling down her chin.

Dec watched, his eyes narrowing. "Is that where she was born, then?"

"No. San Francisco. Why?"

"Just curious. Where's her father? Certainly not one of these guys, huh."

Annoyed at his reference to Larry and Gary, she wiped the spittle from Jacky's chin and put her down on the ground. "So many questions," she said. "Are you investigating my background?"

"Just trying to find out if there's a man on the scene."

She watched as Jacky rolled herself over and began to crawl away, then made a grab for one of the bean poles. "Oh, no, you don't, you little minx!" She grabbed her up again, instigating a wail and cry.

"Lot of work, huh?" He seemed to be waiting for something. "You didn't answer my question. About the man."

"No man. Man in Wyoming."

Dec seemed to be waiting for something more, an explanation. An admission as to whether she was still in love with "the man" or not. She stayed silent.

"So, like, there's a poetry reading down on the beach tonight. Maybe you'd like to come. Does the kid sleep? Or can the queers look after her?"

She didn't like him referring to Larry and Gary that way but supposed it was the word in use. She hefted Jacky into the air once more. "I'll see."

****

There were torches set into the sand, and a huge fire going. Sparks flew out like so many lightning bugs. Joints were passed around, and bongs too. Cassie felt different from the hippies, poets, writers, and artists who sat there. She wished she'd never come down, and then Dec spotted her and waved to beckon her over. She was sorry she hadn't put on a few more layers, with the cool sea breeze blowing in; she hadn't expected it to be this chilly. She sat cross-legged and pulled a thin cardigan about her; her sandals didn't do much for her feet, either.

"You cold?" Dec laughed. He threw his arm around her and pulled her close, then put a finger to his lips as someone got up and began reading.

The voice was resonant but floated out to sea, and Cassie lost some of the words. She tasted her lips, the salt air, the damp, and let the reading lull her. When Dec handed her a joint she took a toke, held it in before breathing out, and then regretted doing that and handed it back.

Dec pulled on it several times and held it her way.

She shook her head no.

"Don't you want it?"

"No."

Someone turned around to quiet them, and Dec continued to smoke on his own. She sat, spread her fingers through the sand, picked up handfuls, and let it fall close to the beach so it wouldn't blow.

She wondered about Coop and if he'd ever seen a beach.

By the time the readings finished, her head had lolled onto Dec's shoulder. He tapped her awake, stood, and pulled her up. He kept her hand in his as he went over to speak with some people, but he never introduced her or them, even when the man said, "Dec, you bring your lady friend over to us for a pig-out one night."

"Great."

Dec led her away, her hand tight in his.

She went with him, not knowing why. She stopped to look at the moonlight on the ocean, a long shimmering white line, a spill of milk on a creased blue tablecloth, the edges zigzagging as the waves rippled. She carried her sandals, dug her toes into the sand and felt its coolness, then released them and followed on.

Dec had a tent in a secluded bit of beach near where the tumble of land met the strand. He'd left a lantern burning so the light through the sheer fabric was inviting, welcoming. He pulled back the flap.

There wasn't much more than an old sailor's trunk with some clothes and records on it, an old wind-up Victrola, and a bedroll spread out with an uncovered pillow.

"Okay?" he asked, as if she knew the question. He started to undress as she stood there uncertain, slightly bent over because of the tent's lack of height. "Come on," he urged her, "take your clothes off."

Unsure of what she was doing, or even why, she followed his instructions, but when he told her to lie down and she started to bend toward the ground, she stopped. It was as if Coop stood in the tent, laughing at her. The idea of having sex with Dec wasn't exactly unpleasant, but it wasn't particularly appealing, either. She wasn't sure why—something about the assumption on his part, the mechanics of it, and the fact she hadn't slept with anyone but Coop.

"You're not very romantic about this."

"Oh, for chrissake, Cassie. You want it as much as I do. Don't play hard to get."

"I'm not, but something resembling a kiss might be nice, a little, you know, cuddle or something." It all flowed through her mind's eye, the way Coop would grab her and kiss her as soon as they were in the bedroom, his seduction of her. Foreplay. And he liked undressing her, letting down her hair if it was up, nuzzling into her neck. She missed that tenderness more than the sex in some ways. She missed Coop.

"Shit, are you kidding me? Cuddling? This isn't a romance. Either you want to have sex or you don't. Which is it?"

Cassie considered this long and hard. She stood there, naked in the lamplight, looking at his body, a priapic pose that somehow excited her. She lay down.

His lovemaking seemed book-driven, as if he held a manual in one hand and was following the instructions. Do this, then do that, push that button, then proceed. His moans and groans were more animal than Coop's had been, more as if he were being tortured than anything else.

When Dec finished, he rolled off her, left her unsatisfied.

"Oh, Jesus, I hope you're on the pill."

"Yes," she said disgusted with herself. "I got it at the Free Clinic in the city." Then she burst into tears.

"Jeez!" He got up on an elbow to look at her. "What the fuck's the matter now?"

She folded herself to kneeling and got her clothes back on.

He let her walk home alone.

The next day, as she worked in the garden, Dec strolled by. He put his hand up in the peace sign and moved on.

****

In August, when Nixon resigned from office, Larry and Gary decided to throw a party. Cassie and Larry elbowed each other in the kitchen and laughed as they prepared food, tossed salads, formed burgers, stuffed vegetables. The scent of fresh herbs from the garden filled the air, and Gary came in to mix several pitchers of mint julep, his version of Long Island iced tea, and margaritas, while keeping one eye out for Jacky, who was trying to pull herself up to stand.

"Won't be long now," Gary noted. "Jacks will be running around, and we'll all be running after her. My dear, we simply must get you a playpen."

"Or a leash," Larry added.

"No, I'm managing." Cassie continued to push stuffing into a pepper. "You've already been far too generous with us. Really," she added, smiling at them both.

"Oh, but we're a family, my dear, a *family*!"

And that, at times, was what she felt as well. She had settled into her life here and didn't miss the commune or the vacillating friends that had come with it. While somewhere in her heart she knew this could not be a permanent arrangement, for now it seemed ideal. Living by the sea was almost as nice as living in the mountains, though she missed that. And missed Cooper.

Yearned for him.

She glanced over at Gary. She thought of him as "Silly Putty" because his face was so pale and round and almost lumpy, a few strands of hair coming down from the back. She realized she had no idea how old the two were, though she figured in their fifties—that's what Dave had said anyway.

Larry was taller, more elegant. His hands had long fingers that seemed to move as if they were boneless. He walked with a stoop, perhaps due to his height, long arms hanging down when he strode about. But she liked him, too, liked the quiet way he inhabited the house compared to Gary's more ebullient manner, more expansive mannerisms.

"Larry, my love, we *really* must get the tables up."

Larry twisted away from the counter to glance at his lover, looked over the top of the glasses that sat on his nose as if they had just landed there. "You can do that. Can't you do that on your own?"

Gary shook his shoulders in a peevish manner. "Well, I suppose, but help is always welcome."

She exchanged a look with Larry. "Come on, then." The two rinsed their hands under the faucet, and she swung Jacky into her arms. They followed Gary to the potting shed, where folding tables and chairs were stored, and each grabbed what they could carry out. She clutched a chair under her free arm and Larry snatched it away.

"You can't do anything holding Jacks. Go on back to the kitchen; we'll do all this."

"Fine." She marched back to the kitchen, settled Jacky on the floor, and got back to preparing a chocolate fondue for the party. When she went to seize an apron off a hook, Jacky wasn't there. In a panic, she looked outside, but the men were still setting up the tables. She dashed to the hall. There Jacky stood, as if it were the most normal thing in the world for her to have walked down the hall.

"She's walking! She's walking!" Her voice was as loud as she could make it without scaring the baby, but she knew the men couldn't hear her, so she dashed to the screen and screamed through that, "Jacky's walking!"

The three adults stood together, arms around each other as if the accomplishment had been miraculous. She pulled away and took a few steps after Jacky in case she fell, but the child seemed stable, diaper-clad, waddling along. Cassie glanced back at the men. Gary had his hands clasped to his chest in total ecstasy, while Larry stood, arms dangling by his side, a small smile on his face.

It was too much for her. It should have been Coop there at this moment. She had denied him this, and all the moments of firsts in their baby's life, every glorious gurgle and giggle, every wonder at the world.

And Cassie sat on the hallway floor and cried.

Chapter Fifteen

The nurse assigned to tweeze out the glass from his face and hands kept shaking her head in disbelief.

"Boy, you really did a number on yourself." She flashed leaf-green eyes at him and a smile that lit her face. She was shapely where Cassie had been thin; efficient and straightforward to Cassie's somewhat unsure dealings with life.

Coop grunted. "What I do on my land isn't anyone else's business."

The nurse put down the tweezers, got some gauze with alcohol, and swabbed the area she had been working on. "You come in here, it becomes our business. What did you think? You could handle this alone?"

"I didn't think."

"No, you sure didn't. I'll say. Could have lost an eye or something, glass flying like that."

"Could have. Didn't."

"Well, aren't you the lucky one." She tweezed another piece, took away the magnifying glass she'd been using, and looked him in the eye. "This was really dumb," she declared.

"Yeah. I'm one dumb bastard. Okay?"

She shook her head. "Cooper Byrnes, huh. My father used to hunt with yours, I think."

He pulled his hand back and looked at it. "You

done here?"

"No. Let me look again. You don't want any bits left in."

"What's your name, then? Or your father's name?"

"Otis Wainwright was my daddy. Barbara Wainwright."

"Oh, yeah, I remember him. Big fellow. Lousy shot, my father used to say." He tried to restrain his lips from turning up.

"Did he, now? Well. My daddy used to say yours was the meanest, cheapest bastard this side of the Rockies."

"Probably was, too. What about it?" He arched a brow at her, waited for an answer.

"You take after him?"

He grunted out a laugh. "Maybe. Then again, maybe not. Want to find out?"

****

They went out a couple of times before Christmas, but he left for Sunny's house alone, not wanting his mother to be involved in any way, after the fiasco with Cassie. More to the point, he didn't want Barbara to intrude on his memories of Cassie that Christmas, when he'd given her the coat and she'd wrapped herself in it and seemed so happy at Hank's house. He held Cassie in his mind as if she were there every moment, what she'd think, what she'd do, what she'd say. No one was going to take that away from him—his memories, his conjuring of her.

But when he came back after New Year's Eve of 1973/1974, he asked Barbara out again.

"Good Christmas?" He drove them into town, to the Wort Hotel for dinner, and thought maybe they'd go on to the bar. The roads were shiny with recent rain. A full moon above gave them a glossy look.

"Oh, yeah. Mother and sisters and all at my mom's house. We all chip in. All women. It's fun."

He stole a glance at her. "What happened to your daddy, then? Passed? Or they divorce?"

"Yep, divorced." She played with the bag in her lap. "Seemed he went to hunt something other than elk, found it, and left for Montana."

He snorted. "Well, I'm a one-woman man, Barbara. Just so's you know." He could sense her studying him in the dark of the car, his face suddenly lit by passing headlights.

"You're a handsome bastard, aren't you?"

"Am I?" It didn't matter to him what she thought, really, nor what he saw in the mirror when he shaved. "Is that on your check list?"

"My check list?"

"Yeah, you know, what you want in a husband."

She was quiet for a moment, considering. "Is that a proposal or something? Isn't it a bit early for that?"

He glanced at her and smiled. "It wasn't a proposal. I just wonder if women size up every man they come up against as potential husband material. Isn't that it?"

"No, that isn't it." She played with her bag some more. "I just think handsome men like you tend to be bastards. So, no, not husband material. But then I'm not looking for a husband."

He snatched a sideways glance. "Good. 'Cause I'm not proposing. I've had my fill of women I thought I'd marry. Date, yes. Sleep with, sure thing. But marry, not on your life."

"All right," she said, snapping her bag open and shut. "I get the picture."

"Just so's you do."

"So when you said you were a one-woman man, you actually meant you were a no-woman man, huh?"

He remained silent, considered this. Maybe what he'd meant was he'd had his one-woman great love and was now finished with love and women other than for…what? Sex? Company?

"I guess I meant I date one woman at a time and don't play the field, but I have no intention of marrying. Okay?"

"I got it. No man I ever met had *an intention* of marrying…until they found someone they wanted to spend the rest of their life with. Funny thing, that."

The truth of that hit him, a sucker-punch. He'd never have thought he would want to marry Cassie, but there it was.

He found parking just opposite the hotel and put his arm around her as they crossed to the restaurant entrance and found a table in a corner.

Barbara sat down, shunted out of her coat, and fixed it over the back of her chair. "So who's hurt you so bad, then?"

"Huh? What do you mean?" He placed his hat on a spare chair and faced her. "Hurt me? How?"

"A woman. It's writ all over you. Boy, you must have fallen hard."

He considered whether honesty was due here and decided it was. "I lived with someone for about nine months. Thought we would make a go of it, but she ran off one day. Left me a note—'thanks for everything.'" He snorted his disbelief, his disapproval. "'Course, she was a lot younger than me and maybe didn't want to settle down yet or something. I should have known better."

"Farm girl?"

"No. Nothing like. Hippie, headed for San Francisco from Boston. Just washed up on the shore one day and stayed with me."

"Jeez." Barbara leaned an elbow on the table as the waitress brought menus. She nodded her thanks to the server. "A hippie. Well, I'll be. I didn't figure you to be that dumb." She waited to see his response but he just played with his menu, waited for more as if it were punishment he deserved. "You really are a case."

"Look." He turned back a corner of the menu and let it snap back. "I don't guess the heart ever knows what the heck it's doing. She was young. She was kind. She did things for me, around the house and all, and there was something about her—something sort of untouched, naïve, you know. Like she was mine to be molded. So I fell in love. I don't know why."

"Is that anything to do with the glass and the greenhouse?"

He sat back and looked her in the eye. "Yeah. Can we talk about something else now? What about you? Pretty thing, late twenties I'd reckon, isn't it time you were married?"

"Yeah, it is. I'm just waiting for the right man."

After dinner, he got them a couple of beers in the bar next door. He had just laid down his cash and turned to hand Barbara her drink when Ty walked in.

"Well, well, we meet again," his ex-friend said.

"I was trying to avoid you, Ty, by coming here. Looks like you got some kind of radar for searching me out." He handed the drink over to Barbara. "This here's Barbara Wainwright. Our fathers hunted together."

"I know you," Ty mumbled. "Seen you over in the hospital after a spill at rodeo. Nurse, right?"

"Right." Barbara bestowed a small smile, almost a sneer on Ty. "You break a bone or something?"

"I can't remember what happened when, whenever I saw you. But I sure as heck can remember you."

Barbara raised her eyebrow at Coop, as if to say, "Beat that."

He slugged back some beer, his glance moving from Ty to Barbara and back again. He wasn't going to compete. Ty could have the woman for all he cared now. "Maybe I should leave you two together. Have a trip down memory lane or something."

"Ooh, aren't we touchy," Ty sneered. "You don't like the competition?"

Barbara peered into her glass, then back at Coop.

"There isn't any competition, Ty. The lady is out with me. You want to ask her out later, you go ahead and do that." He shot back his drink.

Barbara stared at him in disbelief. "Look, I don't know what you two are playing at, what the heck's going on here, but don't either of you take me for granted. I'm not some kid who'll be passed back and forth between the two of you. I make up my own mind who I go out with. I know how to use the word 'No!'"

Coop leaned back against the bar and reviewed her once more, what she'd said, what she was like. "All right," he said at last. "I'm heading home. You want to come? Yes or no."

Her eyes were on Ty when she said, "Yes."

****

176

Their lovemaking was unsatisfying to him. It wasn't that she was inexperienced, but she was lumpish, waited for things to be done to her, unresponsive. He felt as if he were lying with a dead body at times, and at others with some robot on autopilot. He missed Cassie's touch, the way she ran her hands over him, held him. As inexperienced as she'd been at first, she had soon learned to be receptive, giving. With Barbara, the relief that came with his orgasm was brief and unsatisfying, left him wanting something more.

He lay with his arm around her, moonlight slanting in through the window, listened to her breathing for several moments, wondered what she felt and thought.

"You alive over there?" he said at last.

"Yeah, I'm just trying to come down to earth."

He tried not to show his surprise, but he laughed. "That good, huh?"

"Well…you're trying to lay demons to rest. I know that much. But I guess I'm the beneficiary of it."

He sat up and looked at her, then leaned back against the headboard. Barbara studied him.

"I don't want to just be your easy lay, here, Cooper Byrnes. I want you to know that." She sat up next to him, leaning back. "I'm not sure where your mind is. Or your heart, for that matter. Maybe you need more time to heal, to get over her, whoever she was, that hippie gal."

"What makes you think she's still on my mind? I didn't call out her name or nothing, did I?"

"You don't have to. A woman knows when it's not her you're thinking of. Passion like that doesn't often happen on a first time. You weren't thinking of me.

You were desperate to lay a ghost."

****

He didn't call her for a couple of weeks, then heard she'd been seeing Ty. A kind of jealousy rose up in him, annoyance. It wasn't often that a man like Ty would slide in on another man's leavings, so he knew it was Ty playing the old game again, seeing who could win the girl. And Ty's way of getting back at him. Angry, he phoned Barbara again.

"I've missed you," he lied.

"Well. You know where I am and where to find me."

"So, I thought maybe you'd like to go to The Grill."

She laughed. "What's the occasion?"

"Maybe coming to my senses."

"You think you have?"

He guffawed. "Yeah. I have."

"All right, then. I guess the only way for me to find out is to see you again. The Grill, huh? Pretty fancy stuff. When?"

She wore a floral dress with ruffles, heels, a bit of glitzy jewelry, a world away from what Cassie might have worn—adult fashion. He had on a good shirt, slacks his mother had bought him one Christmas but he'd never put on before, and polished boots. For a moment, so uncomfortable in his get-up, he wondered if he should have stuck with Marianne. Maybe he should give her a call sometime. And then he recalled what she'd said that night, that she'd felt he always expected payback, dinner for sex, a movie for sex, and he swore he wouldn't make the same mistake with Barbara.

As they settled onto a banquette, she said, "You

really know how to treat a girl." She smiled, eyes wide, sarcasm in the remark.

"I just thought…I supposed it would make a change. And why not? Don't we deserve it?"

"But it's not your usual thing, Cooper, is it? You proving you're not as tight as your father?"

"My father? Heck, no. I never gave the bastard a single thought. What in tarnation has he got to do with it?"

The waiter came to take a drinks order. He asked for his usual beer, while Barbara settled on an Old Fashioned.

"What the heck's in that?" he asked.

"Whiskey, bitters, and some sugar. You might like it."

"I like my whiskey straight, thanks very much. Whiskey with sugar? Jeez, who the heck invented that?"

Barbara laughed. "Well, it's good. I like it."

"Fine, then. You drink it." He picked up the menus that had been left, handed her one, studied it, resentful of the high prices. "Ca—people can cook better at home for less," he grumbled.

Barbara slammed down the menu. "How do you know? And why'd you bring me here if you're gonna complain about the prices? For chrissake, Cooper."

"Sorry. I didn't mean—"

"Yes. You did." She looked at him long and hard. "You don't have to take me to fancy places if we go out. You want to leave? Now, before we order."

"No. No, I said I'm sorry. Let's have a good time. Have another drink." He beckoned over the waiter for another round and glanced at the menu once more.

"Venison stew. Sounds good. Maybe I'll have that. You want something to start?"

They chatted off and on through the meal, commented on the food, gossiped about people they knew in common, avoided any mention of his ex-girlfriend or Barbara's association with Ty. At the end, he looked over the bill as if he were memorizing it.

"You take that Diner's Club here?" he asked the waiter.

"Yes sir."

Barbara raised her brows. "That bad, huh?"

"No. I just don't carry that kind of money around with me. Easier to carry the card."

A light sleet was falling as he walked her back to his car. He didn't ask her to come home with him that night, remembering what Marianne had said. When he pecked her on the cheek, she seemed disappointed.

"Did I do something wrong?" she asked nonchalantly.

"Wrong? No. Why?"

"Just wondering."

Next day he phoned Marianne.

"I'm getting married, Coop." Her voice was blunt and to the point when she heard him.

"Well, congratulations! That's…that's great, Marianne. Who's the lucky man?"

"I don't think you know him. Name's Bruno Ganph. Montanan I met when I was up there looking for a new cutting horse."

"Well, what the hell kind of name is Ganph? You gonna be Marianne Ganph?"

She giggled. "Guess I am." She hesitated. "You phoning to speak to me or Ty, then?"

"You. Just thought I'd catch up. Well, not so much as catch up as I was going to ask you out."

"Too late. Sorry."

"Me too, Marianne, me too." There was silence on the line before he continued. "Actually, I sort of been seeing someone. You may know her: Barbara Wainwright? Nurse over at the hospital. Local family."

Marianne said nothing for a moment, then, "That the same woman Ty's been seeing? Jesus. You two! I've heard of sharing things, but this is ridiculous."

Coop's anger rose, and he looked at the phone as if it were to blame. "You mean Ty's still seeing her? I knew they'd dated a couple of times but…I didn't think they were still going out."

"Shit." Another long quiet. "He's still seeing her. I didn't tell you that, you understand?"

When he put down the phone, everything fell into place in his mind—Cassie not returning, Marianne getting married, Ty trying to steal his woman, Barbara making him jealous.

Right after Thanksgiving, he bought another, smaller engagement ring from a different shop.

Just after Christmas 1974, he married Barbara Wainwright.

Chapter Sixteen

1975

Seagulls were screaming overhead, and a fat pelican, its long beak jutting out like gardening shears, landed on a rock near the pool Jacky was investigating. It was a warm day for late January, mild with little of the pervasive damp that characterized the Pacific coast. Cassie watched her, the little girl bent over in rolled-up dungarees with matching denim hat, a snug little red jacket, the hat's ruffle shading her face. Everyone here was so generous, they never wanted for anything, especially with Larry and Gary looking after them.

Jacky whirled a stick she had found in the pool and watched sand rise and turn in the water, while Cassie looked on. The child was already covered in grains that stuck to her as if she were being cast in cement. She peered into the pool, shells and stones and fish bones going around in the whirlpool she had created.

"It's too cold now, sweetie. Let's go home."

Jacky turned and jammed a toe on a nearby rock, stubbed it, and looked to her mother for consolation. She started howling her discomfort.

"Oh, now." Cassie swung her into her arms, gathered the toys lying nearby into her bag, and headed back.

"Oh, *there's* the little darling," said Gary as she

opened the kitchen door, baby in arms.

Jacky began to wiggle out of her mother's arms, so she set her on the floor. The child reached up toward Gary, who lifted her.

"Naughty Mommy, letting you go out like that. Far too chilly!" He marched out of the kitchen with the baby.

"Someone rang," said Larry, who seemed to have collapsed on a chair, dishtowel in hand. "The bakery I think. Don't know his name. Need more pies."

She looked at him. "Are you all right?" Her voice held a note of concern.

"Of course I'm all right." He dragged himself to his feet. "Bad night last night. Gary snores like the Old Man and The Sea. Surprised you don't hear him all the way over at the top in your room. So I'm just a bit tired is all."

"Okay, then. Pies, huh? I just baked them a load. How fast are they selling?"

"Didn't you say they take them up to the Sunday market in San Francisco?"

"Yes, but—"

"No buts, darling. The world is your oyster, with those fabulous pies. The whole city goes to that market. I'd bet Cassie's Pies is now world famous. We'll have the hordes come knocking on our door soon, if you're not careful. Bolinas will never be the same."

She smirked. "They're not *that* good."

"Well, they are. You watch yourself. You'll be CEO of an international company before you know it. Pillsbury or some such will come and buy you out, or you'll be another Sara Lee, and then where will we be?"

She laughed. "You're nuts." She gave him a playful tap and left to change. "Be right down."

She stood beside Larry in the kitchen, saying few words since they had baked together so many times by now. Her assistant knew his job, worked on auto-pilot, so the pastry was made, rolled out, pinched, and the berries and sugar measured in no time and with no direction from her.

Larry handed her a large basket of blueberries. "What are you thinking? You're very quiet today."

She stopped, her hands hovering over the berries. "I'm…I'm wondering when you're going to tell me it's time to go."

"Go? Go where? To the bakery?"

"No. Leave. Here. That you've had enough of me."

He gasped and stood back, looked at her as if she had suddenly gone insane.

"Well, for heaven's sake, whatever put that idea in your head? Why would we ever do that? What have we ever done to make you feel that way?" His face creased with sadness and misunderstanding.

She shrugged. "You haven't. It's just, you know." But he didn't know, wouldn't know. And Coop had never really cast her out—it had been her decision to leave. Perhaps she should have sat him down and discussed the situation with him. It was easy to think that now, but she had been so much younger, less mature, less in control.

"No, I most certainly do *not* know! We want you here. You and Jacks are the lights of our poor miserable lives," he exaggerated. "What would we do? How would we survive?"

"I don't know. How did you survive before I

arrived?"

"Well." He turned back to filling the pies sitting out, like soldiers waiting for orders. "I don't know. I don't remember. Oh, my dear. I expect one day you may find a husband and go off and live elsewhere—I expect that will happen. But we'll be devastated. Gary *always* wanted a baby. Always. Didn't he tell you? When his friend told him there was this mother looking for a home with her baby, he was so ecstatic he couldn't contain himself. But if you find a man…well, you must lead your own life, mustn't you."

She snorted. "I wasn't actually looking for a home; they wanted rid of me because of Jacky. In the commune, that is. But I'm so glad *whatever* led me to you two." She stood on tiptoes and pecked him on the cheek. "You two are the dearest." *And would any man want a woman with a bastard child?*

His hand went to his cheek where she had planted the kiss, and he looked down at her, a small conspiratorial smile on his lips. "You'll make Gary jealous if you do that again."

****

She pulled the pies down to the shop in a Radio Flyer red wagon that she shared with Jacky, slow going over the uneven surface of the streets. The pastries were covered to protect them from dive-bombing seagulls that had ruined one the first day out. At the back of the bakery, she was greeted by someone she had never met before—tall, slender, with a shock of ginger hair and a spill of freckles across his nose like lost pennies on a sandy beach. They made him look younger than he was, which she figured to be around her age. Brown eyes, the shade of rich soil, met her with a grin.

"You must be Cassie, of pie fame."

"Well, you have the advantage. Who are you?"

"Carl's brother from Minnesota. Brad Beauchamp." He extended his hand.

She switched the toy's handle to her other hand and shook with Brad. "Minnesota, huh? You escaping the extra cold for the moderate cold?"

"Something like that." His glance shifted to the wagon. "Let me help you with the pies, then. I think Carl wanted them loaded on his truck for the Sunday market up in Frisco."

"*Frisco*, huh? I haven't heard that in a while."

"Well, what do you locals say?"

"Most of us just say San Francisco. Or occasionally we refer to 'over the hill.' Or 'the city.'"

He guided her to the truck and let the tailgate down. She stood with two pies, which she handed over to Brad, who placed them with care in a giant cooler box.

"When do you get paid?"

"Oh. At the end of the month. Why?"

"Just wanted to make sure we don't owe you any money."

"No."

They loaded the rest of the pies.

He leaned back against the truck. "Look. Maybe we could meet for coffee or something. I'm here for the time being. Until I decide what to do."

"Hmm. Decide what to do? Wow. Take hold of your life, huh?" Her one-night stand with Declan loomed in her mind, as well as some jealousy at the notion he could just decide what to do with his life. But then, hadn't she, when she left Massachusetts? And hadn't she when she decided to keep the baby against all advice? And, most of all, hadn't she when she thought so often of Coop but never phoned him?

"Well, if I don't, who will?"

"Well, meeting you would be fine, but you ought to know I have a baby."

"Really? A baby and a husband?"

"Nope, no husband."

"And no lover?"

She snorted. "No lover."

"But you had to have had a lover for the baby—what's its name?—to appear."

"Jacky. Girl."

"Got that."

"Lover in Wyoming. No longer loving."

"Okay. So bring Jacky along one day, and we'll all have coffee, then."

She giggled and started up the hill, the Flyer behind her. When she turned back, he was still there, leaning against the truck, and he waved.

****

He wooed her slowly. She felt as if it were an old-fashioned courtship—meetings for coffee, or a stolen lunch together that morphed into a dinner cooked at the house he shared with Carl, with no attempts made to bed her just yet. He played with Jacky when she was along, took an interest in her, and shared ideas with Cassie as to where he felt his brother's business could go, what he hoped for the future.

"Why do you want to expand it?" They had taken a picnic down to the beach and sat watching Jacky as she sang to herself and dug a tunnel to China. Cassie crunched on a carrot, then bent to Jacky to wipe her nose. "And is it yours to expand?"

"Well. I thought maybe I could get some cash together to go in with him, maybe have a branch up in Frisco. Or over the hill, as you said to refer to the city. You could expand your pie operation."

She crunched on her carrot and chewed for a bit. "I'm not sure I want to expand my pie business. How could I expand it? And anyway, there's a bunch of people starting up an organic veggie farm; that suits me better. Outdoor work, not in some hot kitchen."

"But Larry helps you, you said. Couldn't you expand the pie business with him?"

"No, we do enough. A few pies each day. Makes them more desirable anyway. Plus, Larry can't be depended on. Sometimes he helps, sometimes he doesn't. And sometimes Gary watches Jacky, and sometimes he has other things to do."

Brad sat back against the rocks and took a bite out of his sandwich. "Shit, did you see that?"

"What?"

"Look, look, it's a whale! Coming up for air!"

"Dolphins. We get them quite a bit when the sardines are running."

He glanced at her. "Miss Know-It-All."

She laughed. "I know very little, actually, but I do know we get dolphins here." She crawled over to Jacky and cleaned her face again before realizing a smell arose. "Uh-oh. Diaper change time. Come on."

Brad sat and watched as she got a spare diaper out of her baby bag, lifted Jacky, and put her on a mat to change her.

"Isn't she trained yet?"

Cassie glanced at him over her shoulder, kneeling

to do the change. "I have a potty for her, but she's not shown a lot of interest in it yet. It's really early days."

"A lot of interest? Jeez. If a kid can have someone wipe their ass for them, man, why should they show interest?"

"Well. They get to a point where they want to be grown up, do things for themselves. Then you potty train them."

Brad sighed. "Okay. If you say so." He grabbed a stick off the sand nearby and started making lines through the grains. "How come you use cloth diapers and not those disposables?"

There was a note of resentment in her tone when she said, "Because the landfills will soon be overflowing with disposable plastic diapers. They're not biodegradable."

"Oh. You don't mind getting off the shit?"

She finished the change, snapped Jacky back into her dungarees, and let her get back to digging. "She's my baby, Brad. I look after her, I care for her, I love her. A bit of poop and doing the laundry doesn't bother me."

He blinked at this. "Well, as long as it doesn't go into the organic farm you're so intent on joining."

When she pivoted to look at him, he was smiling.

"Joke, Cassie, just a joke." He tossed the stick away. "Come here, then."

She crawled over and he held her long hair off her face. "You're very beautiful." He pulled her to him, taking possession of her mouth, entangling his tongue with hers, then releasing her. "Maybe you should consider cutting your hair. Seems all the girls are wearing it short these days. Like Twiggy?"

"If you're talking models, then Jean Shrimpton wore hers long, but with bangs. Still, maybe you're right. Maybe a short haircut would be easier to manage."

"Of course I'm right. Just like I am about expanding the pie business."

****

In June, she left Jacky with the men and let Brad take her to see *Jaws* 'over the hill' in San Francisco. They held hands throughout the movie. She occasionally hid her face against his chest when the scary scenes were on. Walking back to the truck he had borrowed, they both tried to imitate the theme music, laughed at themselves. She danced in the streets, unfettered, relieved of her duties as a mother, young again.

They walked past a western-wear shop, and he stopped to look in the window. A sorrow tried to overtake her, tried to thrust through. It was like a sign.

She wouldn't let it taunt her. *Enough is enough. It's been nearly three years.* And she put her arms around him from behind as he gazed into the shop window.

Carl was at his girlfriend's for the night, so when Brad asked her to stay, she just said, "For a little while," and she knew he would realize what that meant. He was a considerate lover and made an effort to please her, his hands finding places she'd forgotten existed, taking his time with her to pleasure her. He stayed sprawled across her after, breathing into her neck, his hand clasped in hers for a while.

"Marry me," he whispered.

"What?" She released herself from under him and

let go of his hand.

Brad got up on an elbow to peer at her. "You can't be surprised. We've been going out for months."

"I know but…"

"I could adopt Jacky and all. We'd be a family."

She sat up, her legs dangling off the bed, her back to him. "It's too soon, Brad. I don't want to rush into anything. Heavens, we just made love for the first time. Plus, we could just live together. Marriage is so…so permanent."

"It's supposed to be."

"I know but—"

"You don't love me."

"It's not that. And anyway, you've never said you love me." She grabbed her clothes off the floor and started to dress.

"Well, I thought you knew. I mean, why would I go out with you if I didn't fancy you?"

His slow courtship and speedy proposal ran through her mind, confused her. "Fancying someone is different from loving them. I fancy a hot dog to eat, but I'm not marrying it."

He scrambled to his feet and found his jeans. "That's idiotic. That's totally different."

"All right. Look. I just need more time. Maybe we could find a place and move in together or something, see how it goes."

"All right. Let's start looking, then."

She sauntered up the hill to the house on her own, turning this around, whether Brad was what she wanted. She knew she'd never stop loving Coop; it had become all too evident. But could she marry someone else, make a life, a family with someone else?

191

A light was on in the kitchen, a welcoming glow until she pulled open the door to see Gary sitting alone, his hands clasped in front of him, moving as if he were toying with an imaginary bit of paper, tears streaming down his face.

"Oh, my God! What's happened?" She rushed to him and stooped to face him, her first thought that something had happened to Jacky.

"It's Larry—he collapsed. The ambulance came and took him away. I couldn't leave Jacky, of course. The lamb is sound asleep upstairs."

"No, no, you must go now. Can you drive yourself? I could bundle her up, and we'll go together."

"Oh, my dear, could we?" He lifted his pale, moonlike face to her. "Would you do that for me?"

"Of course. You get ready, and I'll go up and get Jacky. I'll put her in her carrycot, if she still fits, or you'll have to hold her."

****

The vacant white walls and antiseptic smell of the hospital put Cassie on edge, as if she had entered some alternative world. Larry lay colorless as the sheets that surrounded him, wires and tubes reminding her of the moon walk, as if he were connected to a mother ship. The doctor wouldn't let the baby in the room, so having had Gary hold Jacky so she could go in after his initial visit, she now waited out in the hall while Gary went in once more. In the late night, the halls were dimmed, with a quiet that was more disturbing than peaceful.

Gary stepped out as a doctor entered. "They're going to run tests," he moaned. "Oh, goodness, I hope it's not serious." He turned big damp eyes to her. "I'm so glad to have you here. What would I have done?"

She clasped his shoulder with a free hand. "It'll be all right. He's made of tough stuff." But in her heart she had a premonition, a creeping feeling there were unhappy days ahead.

And she was right. Larry was diagnosed with lymphoma.

They tried to stick to a routine, to keep life as normal as possible, but there was a new normalcy for them now. Gary looked after his partner with a care she almost envied, a sense of missing a love like that. She tried to look after both of them as well as Jacky, and do the pies on her own, too. Brad stopped by occasionally but seemed to be put off by the situation, the smells of sickness, the scurrying to get so much done in a day, the stress, the specter of death. He said he didn't want to interfere or be a nuisance, but she felt there was something more. Occasionally she went down to stay with him, needing the touch of loving that he offered, the feel of someone fully alive.

Jacky did not understand what was going on. She wanted to see Larry and Gary but had to be kept aside by the possibility of infection as Larry underwent his weeks of chemotherapy and radiation and transfusions.

Cassie lost weight. She felt wrung out by it all, ancient. Seeing Larry waste away, a pale globe of a head where once his thick hair had been, tried her ability to keep a happy face.

"You know," said Gary one day, "I think this is worse for you than it is for me. Maybe you need to get away."

"Get away?" The disbelief seeped out of her tone.

"Yes. Get away."

"Leave you? You must be joking."

"I'm not, my dear sweet thing. No use in you ruining your health, as well."

"I'm not ruining my health." She planted a kiss on his forehead. "We'll be fine."

"Oh, my dear. You don't believe that any more than I do, bless you."

One day, while Larry was having his treatment, they went off to buy him the new Sony Betamax system so he could record his favorite programs and watch them when he was able. He loved the game shows— *The Price is Right*, *Jeopardy*, *Wheel of Fortune*, and *Match Game*, and then there was the *Thrilla in Manila* as the Ali-Frazier fight in September was called.

"Why is it that man can speak in rhyme and I can't?" Larry rasped at her.

"You get outta that bed, I'm gonna bust your head; you gotta make a pee, just you call for me; you gotta make a poo, I know just what to do."

Larry looked at her as if she had just landed from another planet and arrived with a second head. "You're crazy, you know that?" He patted the bed. "Come tell me the story of your life. We've never asked who Jacky's father was—is."

She glanced down the hall. Jacky was in a room they had made safe for her to play, a stair gate at the top of the steps. She looked back to Larry and smiled. "Oh. Just someone I knew. Someone I lived with for a while. He didn't want 'any accidents,' as he called it, so when I knew I was going to have the little accident, I left. Left without telling him."

"Foolish girl. No one wants an accident, but when they see a baby, it's a whole different ball game."

"You think so? Well, I overheard him tell his

mother he wasn't going to marry me."

"Did she approve of you?"

"No. Hated my guts. We went for Christmas and had to leave, stayed in a cheap motel, and drove back the next day to kinder people." It replayed in her mind.

"Well, so what did you expect him to say, Christmas and all? 'Yes, I'm going to marry her, hell or high water, and you be damned, dear Mother, and have a merry Christmas too?' Of course, he probably wanted to avoid an argument—"

"Well, he didn't avoid an argument, Larry, because we had to leave anyway." She stood.

"Are you getting peevish with me?"

"Sorry." She perched on his bed once more.

"You're angry because you know I'm right."

"I know no such thing." But in her mind, it occurred to her that perhaps he was right, that perhaps she had misread the whole situation with Coop. She knew him, his ways, his kindness, and yet had decided to read his words rather than his heart.

"Did he treat you well?"

She tried to think. Her days with Coop were fading, and yet they never faded. They were with her always, playing in the background of her life. Had he treated her well? She supposed he had. They'd had their ups and downs, like anyone, but mostly ups. In his own particular way, she supposed he had treated her well.

"I don't know," she told him at last. "I guess he did."

Gary came in with the meds Larry needed and a glass of some concoction said to build his strength. "Your boyfriend is here, my dear. He has the new, fancy labels they've had made for Cassie's Pies. Really something."

"Oh, I forgot."

Larry gave her a weak pat on the back. "You go ahead. We're fine."

She pecked him on the cheek, winked at Gary, and went down the hall, scooping up Jacky as she unlocked the stair gate.

Brad stood staring out the kitchen window, a packet in his hand. He spun around as she entered. "Quite a nice place, really, isn't it? Nicer than Carl's dump."

"Yes. We were very lucky they took us in."

"Us?"

She balked. "Jacky and me. Us. Remember?" She tickled the baby to make her point.

"Oh, yeah. I thought for a moment…I thought you meant something else." He shuffled into recovery. "Anyway, thought I'd bring these over." He held out the packet. "Turned out nice, huh?"

Cassie looked at the little oval labels, "Cassie's Pies" written in a bold script that mimicked her own hand, with the words, "Handmade with Love" underneath. "They're lovely. Really cool." She laughed. "Thanks!" She glanced at him, waiting.

Finally, he said, "You know I meant what I said. That I wanted to marry you. I still do. Maybe we could find a place nearby, work something out. What do you think?"

She leaned over the sink, staring out at the garden, and jiggled the child. "I don't think so, Brad. Not with Larry being so ill and all. It wouldn't be fair to even ask. And I don't think you and I are ready for that. Or at least, I'm not ready for it."

He waited, hung on for something more, a further explanation.

"I guess…I don't know. Maybe I'll never be ready for anything more. Maybe this is all I've got."

Chapter Seventeen

"Well, this is pretty swanky." Barbara watched as the bellman took the tip Coop offered him and left.

"Should be. I'm paying enough." Cooper stood, glanced about at the opulent drapes and chandelier lighting the room like a Christmas tree. "Sure beats going to some sandy beach and sitting for a few days."

Barbara shook her head. "I always thought honeymoons were the bride's prerogative."

"The man wears the pants, sweetheart. Anyway, I could hardly take time to go and sit on a beach. Don't even own a bathing suit. Bad enough leaving Dusty and Hank looking after things for five days."

Barbara started unpacking. "They don't mind. They're being paid well enough, I'd think. And we did postpone the trip for you to get things done."

"Well, isn't San Francisco more interesting? More to do, more to see. We'll have a great time."

"If there isn't an earthquake. Caribbean would have been more romantic, and you know it."

It was difficult showing her affection he didn't really feel, wishing it were Cassie, but he came up behind her, wrapped his arms about her, and gave her a squeeze. "We don't need a beach and sea to be romantic, Barb. We got everything we need—right here." He moved his hand to scoop her breast.

She shook him off. "Well, I hope you're gonna

listen to what I want on occasion, Cooper." She handed him some of his shirts from the suitcase. "Otherwise, this marriage may be going south quicker than your eight-second bronc ride."

He opened a drawer, threw in the shirts, and slammed it shut. Sometimes he wondered if he'd been a bit hasty in deciding to marry Barbara. *Hasty?* Heck, he'd taken less than a second to decide; he hadn't thought it through. And what did she feel for him? She was loving enough and seemed to generally enjoy his company, but was she basing her marriage on that?

He glanced across to her and realized in that moment he didn't feel a thing for her. A finger of disgust with himself chilled him, and he shivered.

Barbara studied him. "You're not catching a cold, are you?"

"Nah." He took more things from the suitcase and put them away. "So what would you like to do, then?"

"Today? We just arrived. After that journey, I think I'll take a nap."

"A nap?" He shook his head. "Barb, how often do we get to a city? On honeymoon? You can sleep later, can't you?"

"Cooper, I'm tired. We didn't have a moment's sleep on that seven a.m. flight out of Jackson. I had the night shift last night. I'm gonna sleep." She waited for his retort. "We'll go somewhere nice tonight, and I'll be refreshed by then."

"You're not pregnant, are you?"

"Pregnant? Heck no. I'm on the pill. I told you that."

Had she been on the pill for a time now? Had she had access because she was a nurse? His mind went back to Cassie and her words that the doctors wouldn't prescribe to unmarried women.

"Great. Fine. You have a rest. I'll see you later. I'm gonna walk around, see the town." He started for the door. "Should I get us tickets for Alcatraz? I understand that's quite an attraction."

"You want to visit a *prison*? I thought them Indians were still there."

"No, Barb, the Indians left a few years back. It's part of the National Park Service now."

"Oh. Well, no, I'm not much interested in seeing a prison. You go if you want to."

"Well, hell. What kind of a honeymoon is that?" He stood, hands on hips, staring at her. "You have a nap. Maybe we can discuss it over dinner, what *we'd* like to do."

But he knew now what he wanted to do, and she had afforded him the perfect opportunity. He stopped at the concierge desk.

"Can you tell me how to get to Haight-Ashbury?"

"Haight-Ashbury?" The uniformed man looked at him in surprise that quickly turned to wariness. "You mean… Sir…" He lowered his voice. "If you're looking for drugs—"

"Oh, for pity's sake." Coop stood back and met the man's gaze. "I'm trying to find an old friend."

"Oh. I see. Have you an address?"

"No. I only know he's living in Haight-Ashbury."

"Have you thought of looking him up in the telephone book?"

"No. Good idea."

"I have one right here. What's his name?"

He hesitated. "Halliday. It's C. Halliday."

The concierge opened the book to the Hs, ran his finger down. "There's a Charles Halliday at—"

"No, that's not it."

"Well, the only other C. Halliday is out in Oakland. None in The Haight here in San Francisco."

Relieved that he didn't have to give away a woman's name on his honeymoon, he just said, "Never mind. I'll go down to this Haight-Ashbury place and ask around. Maybe somebody knows him down there."

"Well, just you be careful over there. There're some crazies walking about. Let me get the map and show you."

****

For an area in a city, he thought, Haight-Ashbury wasn't bad. Victorian houses with bay windows jutted out above the street, a stark contrast to the wide open spaces of Wyoming. There was widespread graffiti, and psychedelic colors on the houses, with sculptures around that stunned him. And hippies, long-haired and ragged to his eyes, everywhere. He could see how Cassie would fit in, remembering her in her bellbottoms, with feathers in her hair, and the mirrored shirt. Where was she now? Had she returned to that life after becoming so different in Wyoming?

He spotted a boutique in which she might have worked or even shopped, and went in to the salesgirl. Heavy black makeup around dark eyes that looked him up and down, the cowboy boots, the Stetson. What did she make of that?

"Sorry," he apologized for no reason. "I'm looking for a Cassie Halliday. She lives around here. I thought maybe you knew her."

"You have a picture?" the woman asked.

"No, no picture. But I have good reason to believe—"

"Believe what you want, mister. A lot of the kids around here change their names, take aliases or nicknames so their parents or the fuzz can't find them. Sorry."

"Okay. Thanks for that." He started toward the door, then pivoted back. "You don't happen to know of any communes I could try, do you? She said she was headed to a commune."

The woman glared at him, running her gaze up and down once more. "Look, who are you, and what do you want? I don't want to be sending some sheriff or someone off to drag a girl back to home in Idaho or someplace when she doesn't want to go."

"No, ma'am. I'm just the idiot who fell in love with her."

"Poor you. Poor girl, too." She bestowed a smile in his direction. "Try the café diner place a few doors down. A lot of the kids go in there to deal. Owner'll be better able to point you in the right direction. Ask for Ben."

Coop touched the brim of his hat. "Thanks. Much appreciated." He returned the woman's smile.

The café was steamy, humid, and there was a momentary silence when he entered, guardedness he felt without ever having said a word. At the counter, three men, in varying hirsute degrees and flamboyant dress, sat and turned to him with interest, all waiting 'til he opened his mouth.

"Is there a Ben here?" Coop spoke to a man, aproned, bald, who had started wiping down the counter with intense interest in his dishcloth.

"I'm Ben. What of it?"

Coop slid onto a stool, wishing he could hand the man some money without anyone noticing, but the other three had their eyes on him. "I'm looking for an old girlfriend of mine, a Cassie Halliday, she's supposedly liv—"

"Left here some years back. No idea where she went. Sorry."

He froze. Something in him hadn't expected any positive information about Cassie; he believed he was wasting his time on a wild goose chase, but here was the evidence Cassie had made it to San Francisco, to Haight-Ashbury, in fact. He recovered himself enough to ask, "She was living in some commune; you don't happen to know which one, do you? Maybe they could tell me more? Or maybe she's still there?"

The man stopped his wiping and studied him. "Might be. But I doubt it. Try the Scott Street Commune. They might know. I'll write down the address."

Shaken, he came out of the café, breathed the fresh Pacific air, and glanced at his watch. It was getting late, and Barb would be wondering where he was, his own nerves making him reluctant to investigate further. What if Cassie were still there, in the commune? What would he say? What would her reaction be to him just turning up on the front doorstep? And married into the bargain. Was it closure he sought? Just a desire to know why exactly she had left? Or was he hoping for something more? With Barb back in the hotel—his wife—what more could there be now?

He took a few steps, unfolded the map in the shade of an awning, and studied it. Just a few blocks. And he knew he couldn't *not* give it one more try.

The house was like the many others in the area, Victorian, not overly well maintained, with a few hippies hanging about. He was an object of curiosity to them all, his western dress being viewed as some sort of costume, no doubt, his clean-shaven jaw and short hair marking him out as not from around here, the combination of the two causing puzzlement and interest.

He wove his way through the kids on the steps and rang the doorbell. He glanced down at the hippies who had moved out of his way, one of whom stood slowly to meet his gaze. The face looked vaguely familiar, creased in displeasure at seeing him.

"You," said the man. He'd grown a beard, and his hair was a lot longer than when Coop had last seen him, the day the hippy van had pulled up at the ranch to collect Cassie.

"Dave. It is Dave, isn't it?"

Dave extricated himself from the group he'd been talking with and came up the few steps to him. "Jeez, man, what are you doing here?"

"I...I just happen to be in San Francisco on business. Thought I'd try to look up Cassie."

"Business, huh. What business is that? Selling dead animals to unsuspecting diners?"

He felt the antagonism, knew right then he'd never get any information on Cassie from Dave—Dave, who had been jealous of him in the first place, who had been in the fight with Ty. He tried to be friendly, realized that was going to be the only way to go. "Listen, you may be right about meat-eating, I don't know—"

"You don't know? You sit out there on your horse

and raise cattle just to kill them, and you don't know?"

He waited, tried to get his own temper under control. "I just thought I'd try to find Cassie, say hello, you know?"

"Cassie's not here. Cassie pushed off some years back. She didn't stay long, left with a man." Dave sneered. "You must know how it is. She picked you up in one night. Now she's picked up someone else. That's how she is."

He felt his stomach tighten. What had he expected? That she would be alone still? That she would welcome him back with open arms? That she had waited for him to show up one day? "I see." His voice was flat. "Is she still in San Francisco, do you know?"

"No idea. And why would you be interested anyway? From what I understand, you're the one who sent her packing."

His face clenched in disbelief. "*I* sent her? No, she ran off. She left a note. I never said a word. I wanted to marry her."

Dave snorted. "A bit late, man, a bit late." He turned to rejoin his friends and left Cooper standing there.

At that moment, he couldn't get down the steps to the street, past Dave and the others. He felt shaky, stunned. He stood thinking it through for several moments, the words he had said to her that morning. He couldn't remember but was sure he had been kind, gentle, going off to buy the greenhouse to surprise her, *what had she thought?* He'd been in love with her, damn it, had bought her the engagement ring. How could she have thought he wanted her gone? Yet it was the same dang thing Hank had said—that Cassie believed he didn't love her. What had he done wrong?

He felt as if he moved in slow motion, gathered himself and made his way past the hippies and back to the hotel. And his wife.

****

The mind is a funny thing. You could try your damnedest to forget something, or someone, but the heart—well, the heart has a mind of its own, as he discovered to his cost.

On their last day in San Francisco, having lunch in an outdoor café, they carried their trays to a large table where other diners sat. Coop put his down as Barbara sat with hers, both of them removing their food items from the trays onto the table. A bit of cellophane had blown over from another diner, and he picked it up to throw away. Then something caught his eye.

Cassie's Pies. Handmade with Love.

He looked across to the couple who shared a small pie for their dessert. "That looks pretty good." He tried to keep an upbeat note in his voice, not anything that would alarm Barbara.

"Yeah, it is." The man spoke with a mouthful. "Sorry about the garbage." He held out his hand for the cellophane, to put it with his other trash.

"Oh, that's all right." He held on to it. "Maybe I'll just go in and see if they have another."

"You want a pie now?" asked Barb in disbelief.

"I'll be right back."

A cashier appeared to be the only approachable person. Sitting at his register, ringing up the items on customers' trays, he had a bored air about him, but leaned over to hear what Coop was saying.

"Do you happen to know where these pies come

206

from? I'd be interested in finding out for my own business," he lied. He held up the bit of cellophane with the label on it.

"Some market or other." The man apparently could care less, so disinterested was he in Coop's enquiry. "No idea. Boss gets in the stuff, I only sell it."

"Yes, but…do you think I could have a word with your boss?"

"On vacation. Two weeks. Come back then."

"And there's no one else who might—"

"Mister, can you move on, please? I got a job to do here."

It was a losing battle. He folded the label twice and stuffed it into his pocket.

****

Their honeymoon had developed into a drab affair for him, simply waiting to get back to Wyoming. Back home, he tried to make the best of his relationship with his wife as Barbara started a routine. Working mostly days except for the occasional night shift she had agreed to, she'd get some dinner ready, which he looked at in his disgruntled manner, ate almost silently, and later sat with her, watching TV. His days went by with hard work, which he followed occasionally with a kind of dutiful lovemaking, a requisite to married life, and more a physical need, more a relief of tension than anything else. He had no doubt that Barbara was happiest on days she had off work when he wasn't around.

By the time Thanksgiving loomed on the horizon, he was sure the marriage wouldn't last. Couldn't last. And he didn't care. He was resentful his mother thought the world of Barb, "a good, decent, local girl who knows our ways," as she put it. It didn't matter that Barbara wasn't any more a churchgoer than he was; she was a westerner, a Wyoming native, and that counted for as much. Sunny remained as pleasant as ever to the new member of the family, but he could tell she knew things weren't right. An exchanged glance, a look his way as if she were checking on him, a sympathetic gaze.

He drove Barb home early Friday after the holiday; she'd told him she had to be back on duty on Saturday night and needed some time to rest up back home. He was locked in his own thoughts and knew she was too. Silence filled the car like the chill outside, a steadily falling blanket of snow that would mute the hills around them, a cold that would dull the senses. The windshield wipers set a steady pace, a metronome to his thoughts. He felt caught, imprisoned in a marriage that was not working, would never work, was not what he wanted.

"You're very quiet," Barb started.

He took his gaze from the road for a moment to look at her. "Well, so are you. You haven't said a word."

"I like your mother."

He grunted. "Well, then, you must have nerves of steel."

She ignored that. "I get the feeling, though, Sunny doesn't quite approve of me. She tried to be friendly enough but, still, I sense she doesn't quite like me."

"Well, I wouldn't know. She never said a word to me about it. Sunny likes everyone. She's that kind of person." And so was Cass. Maybe that was why he'd loved her, she was so open, so opposite to him with his set ways, tight views of people. Maybe that was what she had given him. But he hadn't learned from her, had he? He was still set in his ways, still wanting everything the way *he* wanted it. He'd been at fault with Cassie, he knew; he'd made her think she was unloved. And now he was going to have a failure of his marriage, as well.

He reached across for Barb's hand and gave it a squeeze.

"What was that for?"

"What do you mean? Can't I squeeze your hand?"

"You've never done that, Cooper Byrnes. You hardly show the least bit of affection to me. That's your way, I know that now, but when you give my hand a squeeze of a sudden, I'm a bit suspicious."

He turned to look at her, a crooked smile on his face. "I can't win, can I, Barb? I just can't win."

Part Three: Chapter Eighteen

1976

Little things I should have said and done
I just never took the time
But you were always on my mind
You were always on my mind
     ~Willie Nelson, lyrics, "Always on My Mind"

He sat at the kitchen table, empty beer cans crushed and lying around him, the February blizzard blowing steadily, so that the windows had crystalized designs of snowflakes in every corner, frozen to the panes. Dusty and Hank had left some time ago after helping with the feed and had called him to let him know they'd made it back home safely in the white-out conditions. Barb was on night shift.

He stumbled to the sink, a nausea rising up, then receding as he swayed unsteadily. He yanked open the fridge, looked inside, shut it, the smell of some garlic sausage she'd bought hitting him hard. He opened it again and pulled out some sandwich makings. The new cleaning girl, hired after Mrs. Craven had left to live with her son down in Cheyenne, hadn't been in for several days, and Barb never bothered to do a thing around the house. "We both work," she had said. "You can vacuum just as well as I."

His hands shook as he tossed some ham on a slice of bread, managed to squirt the mustard on, and wondered how his life had gone south so quickly. Who would he leave the ranch to? His inclination to have children had soon faded with the speedy decline of his marriage. It was only a matter of time before they came to their senses and agreed to a divorce. What then? It would be Sunny's kids who got the place, he supposed, and what did they know? Would he ever find someone else? Someone he truly loved? Cassie was a vague ache now, a faded memory, a ghostly presence that only revived when he came across the ring at the back of his sock drawer. He'd pull it out, snap open the little box, look at it, turn the ring to read the inscription before he put it back in, and snap the box shut again. Then he'd throw it back behind some socks until the next time.

He ate at the sink, the bread so dry in his mouth it almost made him gag. He rinsed the plate and left it on the side, twisted around to regard the discarded beer cans sitting there and decided to leave them 'til morning. As he started for the stairs, they bothered him again, and he realized they would only raise Barb's ire. He grabbed a bag and, with one swift movement of his arm, shoved them all in, tugged the ties closed, and flung the bag into a corner.

Later he wouldn't remember lurching up the stairs to bed.

****

Cassie felt as if a part of her had died, as if atoms of her soul were being cast out into the sea. Gary and she stood on the shore, Jacky's hand in hers as they let Larry's ashes fly out on the wind. So much of the last year had revolved around caring for him. A shower of the ash came back at them, carried on the sea breeze, catching on their skin and in their faces. Jacky started to fuss, swatted at the ash and stuck her tongue out to spit. She wore a little red tartan dress, in stark contrast to the blacks and grays of the mourners around her, her dark blond hair pulled back into two ringlet pigtails, curls jiggling on either side of her head as she tossed around.

Gary looked at the urn he held, obviously decided they'd let go enough for Larry's wish to be satisfied. He held it up to the surrounding crowd, swung away from the shore, and led the group back up to the house, a Pied Piper in mourning. Cassie stayed by his side with Jacky.

It never ceased to amaze her how they had become a family, the four of them, with such feelings of closeness to one another. Maybe that had been why she left Coop—because something in her told her she would never have that feeling with him. Yet as she marched with Gary to the house, she recalled how he had been in the evenings when he wasn't otherwise occupied, how he had made love to her, bought her things as tokens perhaps of love. Had she been harsh on him? Misunderstood?

She had cooked up a feast for the wake, dishes and bowls of food strategically placed on the large dining room table they had rarely used for the time she'd been with them, a stack of plates, napkins, and flatware. In the kitchen, she had set out glasses and an array of drinks for people to help themselves. It seemed all of Bolinas was here, plus many from San Francisco, from the clubs they had once frequented, gay bars, friends they had known since moving to California.

"My dear one, we must speak." Gary found her

alone, getting more food from the fridge to replenish dishes. "The lawyer is here, our lawyer, and he wants to discuss the will."

"But surely that doesn't concern me." Cassie stopped what she was doing, perplexed. "I'm sure it's meant to be private to you."

"Oh, no, you see—"

Brad came in carrying Jacky. "She says she wants to wee-wee. I don't think I'm quite qualified yet, am I?"

Cassie glanced from one man to the other. "No. I'll take her." And she lifted her daughter from Brad's arms and set her down, took her hand and headed off to the bathroom.

****

Something had woken him from his drunken slumber, fully clothed, passed out on his bed, boots still on. He opened one eye slowly, vaguely aware of a rapping sound. He lay there conscious that something was strange. A blue light, regular as a heartbeat, flashed across the room. Its aura of carnival was in direct contrast to the pounding in his head. He sat up slowly as the knocking got louder.

"Hang on," he rasped.

"Mr. Byrnes! Mr. Byrnes! Cooper Byrnes!" Voices drifted, muffled by the snow and wind, as if his name had come up on some registry for the grave. *Your turn, Cooper Byrnes!*

It took him a couple of moments to get himself together, pull himself to his feet, and practically fall down the stairs. Sheriff's deputies had already entered his kitchen, stomped their feet, and held their hands to the warmth from a ring they had lit on the stove.

He stood in the doorway, grizzled from sleep,

unshaven. "Make yourself at home," he grumbled. He recognized one of the officers, a man from a ranch on the other side of Jackson, with whom he'd gone to high school. He nodded to him. "Gordy. What're you doing here?"

Gordy looked at him, embarrassed. His colleague snapped off the gas. "I don't know how to tell you this, Coop." His voice was low, apologetic.

"Well, spit it out. No use holding it in, then."

"It's Barbara. Your wife was in a car accident. Went off the road. Skidded, we think, on the ice."

"Shit. Where is she now? Hospital?" He glanced at the clock on the wall, took it in that it was still only eleven o'clock and wondered how she'd gotten off early. The fact she was in hospital, hurt, only slowly sank through his alcoholic haze. Dulled by it, cheated, it was another problem he'd have to deal with.

"I'm afraid she's gone, Coop. DOA. There wasn't anything they could do."

He sat down. The news washed over him, as if it were about someone he knew only distantly, and then it began to make its way through. Nothing sobers you quicker than bad news, he thought. He ran a hand through his hair and looked back at Gordy. He tried to reach into himself but felt nothing because nothing was what he had felt for Barbara.

"There's more, I'm afraid." The officer stepped from foot to foot, as if some dance were about to start.

"More?" He glanced up at him, puzzled. "What the hell more can you be telling me than my wife's dead, Gordy?" Still, the timing was running through his head, *she should have been at work, at the hospital 'til midnight. Why was she out on the road?*

Gordy took in a deep breath. "She wasn't alone. Ty Hart was driving. We're fairly sure his blood alcohol was above the limit. Car had discarded bottles in the back, like…well, you know…they'd been having themselves a little party." He waited for a response, but Coop just stared vacantly at him. "I'm sorry."

"Well." He rose to his feet, realized he wasn't surprised. "Is Ty gone, too?"

"Yes, sir. Car did several flips before landing. They weren't wearing their seatbelts. Makes you think."

"Gordy, it makes me think about a lot of things, but those damned seatbelts are pretty far down the line."

He watched them go, shut the door on the cold, closed it on the life he had somehow made for himself. He wouldn't have ended his life with Barb this way for anything, but he wanted something more, something Cassie had given him, something maybe only Cassie could give him because, as he now knew, she had loved him. Looking back, he could see how she had slowly been changing him, wheedling her way into his heart, making a home for them here. And he'd never had that with Barb and would never have that again.

****

"*Fifteen thousand dollars*?" Cassie held her clasped hands against her chest, wide-eyed and open-mouthed. "But why?"

"Oh, my dear one, you've done so much for us, for him in his last days, always cheerful, always there when we needed you. I don't know *how* I could have managed, and Larry and I discussed it and just felt it was right. Anyway, he's left me more money than I'll ever spend in my lifetime, and I've the house to sell and that ludicrous Custom Cruiser Wagon of his—"

215

"You're going to sell the house?" Cassie felt her life change in that moment, that the tide of her life was going down a different river. She was being forced to start making decisions and find a new direction for both herself and Jacky, who would soon start proper school.

"I'm thinking of it. It has so many memories for me—we've lived here forever, it seems. And as much as I hate to lose you and little Jacks, it may be time for me to move into the city where I'm closer to—well, others, other friends of Larry's and mine. And I think I'd like to go home for a bit, as strange and unwelcoming as it may be."

"I thought this was your home."

"Nebraska, dear one. Harrison, Nebraska, to be exact. About as small a town as you can get. I think the population is less than two hundred, so you can see why I had to leave. Not exactly 'gay central,' is it? Actually, I don't even think they realized what I was, so small and isolated a place as it was. Is. Near the Wyoming border, as well."

"Hmm."

"Hmm?"

"Well, I was only thinking 'Wyoming.' Jacky's father is there. But he probably doesn't even remember me now. I mean, I have a reminder of him, but what was I to him? Someone he slept with?"

"I doubt that's all you were. You make him out to be something…something unpleasant, dear one, and I'm sure if you loved him he wasn't. Couldn't be, if you cared for him so much and stayed with him nine months, didn't you say?"

"Yup. Nine months."

"He hasn't forgotten you." There was finality in his

voice. "Goodness, who could forget you anyway?"

Cassie gave Gary a hard hug and stayed for a moment with his arms around her. "He's probably married by now anyway. He was—is—seven years older than me. Anyway, I can't take that money. It isn't right."

Gary released himself to hold her by the shoulders. "You can. And you will. Larry will turn in his grave if you don't."

"Larry isn't *in* a grave."

"Well. His ashes will fly out of that blasted urn and douse you if you don't take it. Go fly that Concorde thing to Europe, have a giant vacation, have fun."

"I don't think so. Maybe it's time for me to visit home as well."

"Boston? Well, Nebraska is on the way. What say you if we have a little road trip, the three of us. You drop me in Harrison and take the car on to Boston, then. I'll gift it to you for sharing the driving."

"Really? I love that woody."

Gary rolled his eyes. "It's yours, then, dear one. I just have to at least make the arrangements to sell the house, and then we're off." He hesitated a moment. "But what about Brad, may I ask? I thought you two were sort of a thing."

Her lips turned down, and she felt embarrassed. "I think it was more his thing than mine, really. I don't know. Maybe the break will do us good, let me figure what my feelings are. And then if I come back…"

****

Cooper stood by his wife's grave, her family on the other side saying their last farewells. There'd been a thaw, and the ground was slushy, slippery. He watched as his mother clung to Sunny's arm as they made their way back to their car. Suddenly, he turned, and Marianne was at his elbow.

"I thought you might have come to Ty's funeral. You were best friends most of your lives, no matter what he may have done at the end."

He met her gaze with his own. "And I prefer to remember him that way, Marianne—the days we were a roping team at rodeo, the days we went out together, taking bets as to who could get which girl, having a few drinks together. Not the way he ended up with my wife in the back seat of a car."

Marianne nodded her acquiescence.

"You happy then, Mrs. Ganph? Things turn out all right for you?"

"Things have turned out very well for me, Coop." She patted her stomach.

"When's it due, then?"

"April."

"April. Well, I'll be. Good for you."

She hesitated before saying, "I'm sorry things haven't worked out well for you this far, but your life's not over, you know."

He started back to his pickup, gave Hank a wave as the other stood by the truck. "No, things aren't over for me. Yet. But I doubt I'll marry now. I had one great love, I guess. Didn't know it at the time, of course, fool that I was."

Marianne stopped and studied him for a moment. "Not me, I hope."

"No, sorry, not you."

"And not Barbara, by all accounts. Who, then?"

He grunted out a laugh. "Oh, well. I think that's

gonna have to be my little secret."

They strolled together a few moments, but right before they reached the cars, Marianne stopped and faced him once more. "Surely not...not that girl you lived with? The young girl? We all thought you were crazy."

"Yep, crazy as a jay bird. Most crazy for letting her go." He pushed his hat back a bit and bent to peck her on the cheek. "You know, it's the damnedest thing. I don't think I really knew I was in love with her at the time. I'd decided to marry her, but even then... Guess I just took it all for granted. Well, anyway. The heart is a funny ol' thing, Marianne. You hold on to Ganph and what you got, 'cause you sure as hell don't realize what you have until it's gone."

****

"I'm still in love with you. I still want to marry you."

Brad stopped and reached for her hand. Sand hit their skin with a biting sting, and Cassie released herself to bend and give Jacky's face a wipe.

"I'm going to go with Gary, drive to Nebraska, then Boston, and see what I feel. I think I need to get away for a while. I just don't know what I feel after all this—Larry's death and all. And I have to decide where I want Jacky to grow up, to go to school. I'm not sure Bolinas is it, Brad, it's so...so insular. Then again, I seem to be attracted to places like that."

"But you've made a life here. The pies, and the gardening, and all. And—I had thought—me."

She tried to keep the wonder from her face, or the distancing. Already she could feel the space between them, the completion of their relationship. Yes, the distance she felt from him. It puzzled her why she should love Cooper but not Brad. What was it that led the heart to one person and not another? Even if that other was there in front of her and wanted her.

Jacky pulled away to inspect a pool of water in the sand, and the two adults stopped to watch.

"I guess…" Brad stopped, looked embarrassed, alone.

She smiled at her daughter, who put her hands down into the pool and grabbed them back from whatever demon she saw there. "I guess you guess I don't love you, Brad. Is that it?" She twisted toward him and then back to her post and watched her daughter. "No, and I'm sorry. If I could, I would. I tried to. I really tried. You've been so good for me, to me. And to Jacky. But I just don't feel it. Maybe it was looking after Larry for so long that dulled my emotions, and maybe the time away will…well, you know what they say: 'absence makes the heart' and all that. Anyway…" She spun back toward him. "I'm bored with the pies. It's really time for me to find something I want to do with my life, something that insures Jacky's future, and I don't think it's here."

"We could find it together. I said I'd adopt her. I'm happy to do that. For you."

"I know you are. But I don't think I can have one man become her father when her real father isn't even aware she exists. I just…I don't know if that's fair for either of you, and certainly not to Jacky. Maybe I need to tell him once and for all, have closure on it, give him a chance to be a part of her life. Maybe he's not interested and would say she wasn't his. I have no idea. Yes." She stared at the ground as if all the answers were written there, in the sand. "I need to see about that, have closure on it, and be able to get on with my life without Cooper Byrnes hanging, always there, present, in the background."

****

The door creaked open, and Hank stuck his head in.

"I'm sober. Sober as a judge." Coop held out his cup of coffee and nodded to the glass pot on the coffeemaker to see if Hank wanted a cup.

Hank's face stretched in a wide smile as he came in, poured himself a mug, and held it up in a toast. "Three weeks, then. How does it feel?"

"Well. The evenings are killers, but somehow I get through. Mornings are great. I feel like a new man, but I'm not sleeping very well, so I don't know how I feel so good."

"You'll get into a routine, I reckon. You'll sleep."

"Yeah, well. I don't want to have to take any of them sleeping pills. Mogadon or what have you. Seems like it'd be jumping from the frying pan into the fire."

"You don't need drugs, Coop. You just need time."

"Well. I guess I got plenty of that." He downed the remains of his coffee, rinsed the cup, and set it on the dish rack. "Okay, let's head out."

Chapter Nineteen

The parting with Gary was brutal. Despite the age difference, his mother thought Cassie was his girlfriend and shed her own tears to see the 'lovers' part, her gnarled hands shaking as she dabbed away the wet from her pleated cheeks. Gary, of course, cried buckets; every time he stepped away as a final farewell, he came straight back to her, as Jacky howled her chagrin. Cassie blubbered but tried to be the one to put on a brave face, though brave faces weren't in her résumé.

"You will come and see me, dear one. Oh, please say you will. Back in San Francisco. When I'm settled?"

"Yes, yes, of course. And I'll write. You write. You must." She lifted Jacky to give him one last kiss on his damp cheek before she finally pulled away, shaking with the letting go, and strapped Jacky into her little booster seat. A quick glance at the map, and they were off with a last wave. Gary stood in the street, bawling, as his mother waved her hankie.

She wasn't sure whether they would reach Jackson that night. Jacky's needs to stop, her claims she was carsick when she wasn't—just to see if her mother would halt the car, then giggling when Cassie hurriedly pulled off—lengthened the journey. Lusk, Lost Springs, Orin. They stopped for a break in Douglas, a couple of curiosities in the Depot Restaurant, but she ignored the looks. Glenrock, then Casper was a proper town and warranted another quick break. Moneta, Shoshoni, Crow Heart. The baby was asleep, napping, so she kept going, ignoring her hunger, right through the Wind River Reservation. The plains opened out like spread hands, empty palms, shades of russet and pale yellow abruptly meeting the wide sky, popcorn clouds going off into infinity. Exhausted, she stopped in Dubois, a sense of coming home spreading through her like swallowed medicine. Through the Bridger-Teton National Forest, into Moran Junction…and home.

Home. That's how it felt. In the depths of her heart, she felt she'd come home, with Jacky gurgling and chatting and singing in her little seat, even in the dark that now greeted them as they passed the antler arches of the town square and parked outside The Wort.

She tried to hold onto that feeling of home, but the night in the hotel made it all seem foreign once more. The noise from the saloon downstairs drifted up, and the rhythm of the swinging doors seemed to be saying, "Why, why, why, why." And *why* was what she asked herself all night. Why had she come? What did she expect to accomplish? Did she really wish to lay to rest the constant specter of Cooper Byrnes and her memories of him? Or was she hoping—foolishly—for something more? Why was she lying to herself? Or was she? And could she even face him?

In the morning, after they'd shared breakfast in the restaurant downstairs, she managed to arrange for a babysitter to look after Jacky for a couple of hours. Jacky was not pleased, and howled at her departure. No doubt the memory of recently leaving Gary was painful to her, scaring her that her mother might follow suit.

Her bottom lip quivered with the news, until Cassie made sufficient promises of candies and treats upon her return.

Not a lot had changed in town; a few more shops were spread along the road now, but nothing substantial. Driving out to the ranch past the development called The Aspens, she could see more houses were going up, some condos. But the mountains were as they ever were, ragged peaks, iced even on this late August day. There was a hint of autumn in the air, the first yellows of aspen leaves, an early chill wind.

The ranch looked deserted as she drove in, but of course, she realized, Coop might well be out. Would be out. Another car, a somewhat beat-up Chevy, was parked outside next to what had been her garden plot. She stared at it a moment, the fencing gone and in its stead what looked like a cement base to some building. She gazed at it, wondered if Coop had planned to build something there, and what it might be. Then she knocked on the door.

"Hello?"

There was no response, so she opened the door a couple of inches and called again. The sound of a vacuum greeted her, and she thought it would be nice to see Mrs. Craven, so she went in. Nothing inside had changed; everything was in the same spot as if she had left yesterday.

"Hello? Mrs. Craven?" She stood at the bottom of the stairs. The vacuum stopped. *"Hello?"*

A young Latina woman came to the top of the steps, looked down at her, a mix of worry and confusion on her face. "Mr. Cooper not here." Her speech was heavily accented.

"Oh." Cassie hesitated. "What happened to Mrs. Craven?"

"Not here."

"I see." It occurred to her that she wasn't going to get much out of the woman if she didn't speak English well, since her own Spanish was not good either. "*Donde es Señor Byrnes, por favor?*"

"Not here. Later."

She swallowed a breath. "I see." How stupid had she been? Thinking she could find Coop at home in the middle of the day, and what did she think she would say to him? *Hello,* and *You have a daughter*? She felt trapped, unable to let him go because he had the right to know, unable to face him. And if he was married, what then? What would his wife think or feel?

She sauntered back into the kitchen, heard the vacuum start back up, and stood, tears laying tracks down her face. By the phone was the pad and pencil he kept there. She jotted down her mother's Boston address and phone number, nothing more, and left.

As Dusty once said, the ball is in your court, Coop.

****

Cooper got home late, a sick cow having given cause for concern. He'd waited for the vet to show up, and bedded down the animal in the barn. He found he was happiest, anyway, when he was tired, didn't think about having a drink, just got together some dinner, watched a bit of TV, and went to bed. As he entered with the dogs, he let the screen slam shut behind him, but they started to yowl and rushed around as if they were looking for something, sniffing every room.

"Well, what in tarnation has got into you two today? It's just Maria, for heaven's sake." He toed off his boots, checked the money he'd left for the housekeeper was gone from the kitchen table and the place looked clean. He washed his hands in the kitchen sink, grabbed the towel, and headed to the fridge to feed the dogs and get out a cooked chicken he'd bought the other evening when doing his grocery shopping.

Staring at the bird, he decided he was too tired and hungry to heat it, and had started to pull off a leg to just eat standing there when the phone rang. He gave another quick rinse to his greasy hand before he twisted toward the phone hanging on the wall—and stopped. The pad that hung there had something written on it. Puzzled, he picked up the phone and stared at the writing. A bold yet childish, familiar hand.

"Coop, it's Sunny. I just rang to tell ya Mama's feeling better. Her temperature is down, and... Coop, are you there?"

He swallowed, never took his gaze from the pad, frozen in that moment, not sure whether he was kidding himself, lying to himself, or if what he thought he saw was actually there. "Yeah, I'm here," he finally mumbled.

Sunny faltered. "Coop, are you all right? I just rang to tell ya—"

"Yeah, I heard you, Sunny. You rang to tell me Mama is getting better. Well, that's great, just great."

"You haven't been drinking again, have you, Coop?"

"No, Sunny, I haven't been drinking. I don't think."

"Well, what the heck is that supposed to mean?"

"Nothing. It was a joke. I gotta go. I just walked in, I'm exhausted, and... I gotta go." He put the phone back on the receiver and stared at the piece of paper. It couldn't have been there for four years and he'd never noticed it. Was it some kind of prank? But who would do that to him? He stared at it once more, picked up the phone again, and dialed the number.

After nearly ten rings, a woman answered. *Crotchety* is what he would call the voice that came down the line.

"Do you know what time it is?" she began. "Who is this?"

"I…I wonder if Cassie Halliday is there, please? I'm sorry if I woke you, but it's urgent."

"Urgent? She's not been in an accident, has she?"

"An accident? Oh, Jeez, I hope not. I'm sorry. She left me a note with this number. Do you happen to know where she is?"

"No idea. She rang me from a hotel in Wyoming last night, said she was on her way home, hoped to make Nebraska or Iowa or some such godforsaken place by nightfall tonight or, if she stayed on, she would ring me again and let me know. Well, she hasn't rung, so…"

He stood, the receiver in his hand. She'd been there. She'd been in the house, written the note and left. Left Jackson, too. His mind cycled through it all.

"Oh, for heaven's sake." The phone went dead.

As the hours passed, he went through his routine like an automaton, mindless as to what he actually did. The dogs were now quiet, so he must have fed them. He got out of the shower, not sure if he'd washed his hair, felt it was wet, and decided that was proof. His bedside water ended up on the floor, and he wasn't sure if he'd brushed his teeth, so he went back and found he'd left the toothbrush with paste on it by the side of the sink. Sleep didn't come as he went through it all in his mind once more. She was obviously driving from California to Boston and had stopped in Jackson to see him—which wasn't the most direct route, so she must have *wanted* to see him—and was back on the road headed home. Depending on how fast she drove, she could be home in Boston anywhere between three and five days, he figured, unless, of course, she stopped somewhere else to visit or whatever, and took longer. If he flew, he could be in Boston the same day. Then what would she say?

Why hadn't she stayed to speak to him, if she'd been here? Had she stopped just to say, "Hello, how are you?" Had she thought it would be a fun thing to do? Maybe she wanted to apologize for leaving the way she did. It was nearly four years, four long years to him, and he tried to imagine what she was like now, what had happened to her in that time. Had she changed, was she different, had she been hurt, married, what?

Well, Coop, you're not gonna find out just lying here, are you?

In the morning he phoned the airline and got a ticket to Boston a week away. When the agent on the phone asked about his return, he told her to leave that open.

Chapter Twenty

Coop had the sense of being confined in the rental car, as if he wasn't getting enough air to breathe. It was too small, after driving pickups his whole life, and city traffic seemed to be faster than what he was used to. He hadn't driven outside of Wyoming, Idaho, or Montana for years now, and he felt everything coming at him at once. Every so often, when he found a place to pull over, he would park at the curb, look at the map the rental company had given him, try to memorize the names of the roads, and proceed once more. He was getting frustrated. He had been up since early morning and with the time change, the stopover in Denver, and the lack of sleep, was wound up. Probably too much to deal with, he thought, excitement at the possibility of seeing Cassie again. He hadn't even checked into the hotel he'd booked, The Fairmont; somewhere in the back of his mind had been the idea he would whisk Cassie away to spend the night with him. *Fool. Dang fool*, he thought to himself. *One step at a time.*

When he found the street, he marveled that she was brought up—as he figured—among these little brick houses, stoops leading up to front doors, some of them two-family, by the look of it. Enclosed. Claustrophobic. No sky. Streets where the kids had to play, where they rode bikes down the middle, with vehicles avoiding them; some children kicked balls around and stepped aside as cars drove by. A few little girls played jump rope on the sidewalk; old ladies sat out on the steps watching.

He pulled up in front of number fifty-seven and gazed up at the quiet house, the front door apparently open to the screen at the front. For a moment, he sat in the car, nerves tingling, as if he had waited for this every moment of every day for the past few years, his body suddenly aching to see her again. He took a breath, neatly folded the map, and pushed it into the glove compartment before he lifted his Stetson from the passenger seat as he swung out of the car and strolled around to stand in front of the house. He was aware of curious glances, a momentary hush from the kids before they proceeded with their games once more. He strode up the steps to the front door and rang the bell.

"*Jacky*! See who that is for Nana, will you, sweetheart? Don't open the door, though." He thought he recognized the voice from his phone call: Cassie's mother? Nana? Who was Jacky? Did Cassie have a sister with a child? No, she had no sibling, did she?

A little girl appeared on the other side of the screen, head bobbing like a daffodil in the breeze, her two pigtails swinging as she stretched her neck up to gaze at him.

"Hello," he said. He couldn't help but grin, something inside of him letting go. "Who are you, then?"

"Who are *you*?" she retorted quick as a flash. "Are you a cowboy?"

"Yeah, I am. I'm Coop. I'm a friend of…of Cassie's. Is she at home?"

"Mama's not here. She went to buy groceries, but

she'll be back soon. She said so."

His heart rolled up, tight, wary. "Mama? Cassie's your mama? What's your name, then?"

"Jacky."

"Jacky? That's a pretty name. Jacky what? Jacky…Halliday?"

"Jackson *Byrnes* Halliday," she corrected him, hands on hips.

"Jack—" The world seemed to stop then. Coop slid to his knees, his hands skimming down the screen as if he would touch her, as if she were a baby and he was viewing her through hospital glass for the first time. "Well," he managed to stutter out, suddenly unsure of his place in the world, "isn't Jackson a boy's name?"

"That's why Mama calls me Jacky, silly."

"I…I see." His hand somehow managed to find his forehead, and he rubbed it. "So how old are you, then?"

"I'm three." She shook her head, a pride in her age.

"Three years old," he whispered. "Why, that's a lovely age."

She looked at him strangely. "Why are you crying?"

"Oh, I…I guess I have something in my eye." He swiped at his face, tilted his hat back, saw his face in hers.

"Who *is* it, Jacky?" The grandmother's voice shouted from another room.

"Mama's friend!"

"Well, tell her she's not at home, to come back later."

"Nana says—"

"I heard your nana, sweetheart. I'll just wait on the step, if that's okay."

He felt numb, boneless, chilled. He could hardly make it down to the step where he sat, chin in hand, and tried to catch his breath, his sight swimming. All this time. All this time and he'd known nothing. She'd kept it from him, kept the child from him, and why? When he'd been prepared to marry her, *wanted* to marry her, to have her with him always. Anger fought with sadness, a sadness so deep he felt its poison in his veins and couldn't think straight. He tried to remember their last days together—that Christmas at Sunny's when he left with her because she wasn't welcome, then going on to Hank's for the dogs and having Christmas with him. She'd mentioned heading to California, and he'd said nothing, but went out for the greenhouse and bought the ring, and she'd been gone. And the doctor appointment. Had she found out then? Was that it? Or had she known, suspected, and that was why she'd insisted on driving to Idaho on her own. Why hadn't she told him? It all played over and over and over in his mind.

A large station wagon pulled in behind his rental. He could see her release her seatbelt, turn slightly to get her handbag, and extract herself from the car. She went around to the back to get out a bag of groceries, unaware of being watched until she shut the wagon's rear door, hoisted her handbag onto her shoulder once more to hold the groceries better, and turned toward him.

How much older she looked, no sign of the young hippie now. Grown up. A ladies' handbag on her shoulder and normal clothes, short hair. Almost professional-looking, mature. A mother.

She froze.

He stood, the moment stagnant like a memory, each staring at the other, hardly breathing, until Cassie shook her head and took a few steps up the stoop and set her groceries down.

"Why didn't you tell me?" It wasn't how he meant to start, but those were the words that tumbled out of his mouth, as if a dam had burst its gates. "Why didn't you tell me, Cass? All this time…all this time I wondered why you left like that, that day. I went out to buy you a greenhouse, and I bought you an engagement ring, was going to ask you to marry me, and I came home to find that note, both your notes, and you gone, and Hank saying he'd taken you to Hoback and seen you off—and all this time, all this time, not a single word. Didn't it ever occur to you I had a right to know? Didn't you ever think for one moment that I might want to be a part of her life, Jacky's life, that I *wanted* to be a father, that I wanted to *marry* you?"

"Marry me? *Marry* me? I heard you tell your mother you weren't going to marry me, Coop. I heard it!"

"How many times did I say to you I don't like people butting into my business? How many times?"

"*It was your mother!* And all I ever heard from you was, 'Go on the pill, Cassie. We don't want any accidents,' time and time and time again: 'See a doctor and go on the pill.'"

"Yes. Because I knew, as sure as night follows day, one day you were going to hightail it outta there. You kept saying you were going to California. You were still thinking about California, even at Christmas at Hank's, and if that's what you wanted, I wasn't going to hold you back. So why would I want you having my child? I wasn't going to stand in your way. And sure enough, what happened? You went and picked yourself up one day and just walked out, just like I thought you would."

"If you thought that, why did you build a greenhouse? Why, as you say, did you buy a ring? Why did you never say—just once, Coop, just *once*—that you loved me?" She reached in her pocket to find a tissue and gave her nose a wipe, with a swipe at the tears.

Coop reached into his own pocket and brought out his own handkerchief, along with the ring, still in its box. He opened it, took the ring from its slot, and handed it to her. "What does it say? Can you read it?"

Cassie turned the ring in her hand and peered at the inscription on the inside. "Love forever, 1973." She was sobbing now, crumpled down onto the step below him. "You never said. Not once, Coop, not a single word about love, or to ask me to stay. Nothing. What was I supposed to think?"

"What were you supposed to think? You were supposed to think I did everything to please you, every last damn thing, from buying you…oh, seeds to plant and the blasted pressure cooker, to fencing out that land and teaching you to ride, and always trying to make it up with you when you were angry, and ending my friendship with Ty after some twenty-odd years."

"Ty? Ty! It was Hank who pulled him off me and told you what an animal he was!"

"Yeah, and then I came in and told him to get out. I didn't know what the hell was going on. What am I, a fortuneteller, a seer? I didn't walk in until Hank had got Ty off you."

"Mommy!" Jacky's voice bellowed out from the house.

"Just a minute, Jacky, I'll be in, in a bit. Mommy's talking, sweetie." She held the ring still, unsure of whether she should hand it back, put it on, or throw it in the street. "Did you even try to find me? Ever?"

He stood for a moment, uncertain of whether the truth was right. "Not immediately, no. I thought if you had left, then you didn't want to be with me, that you wanted to go. And then a couple of years later I was in San Francisco—"

"*You were in San Francisco?*" She was stunned.

"On my honeymoon."

"*You're married?*"

"Oh, good Lord, Cassie, no…no." He seemed to crumple onto the step. His hat removed, he put his head in his hands, ran his hands through his hair, and looked at her. "I married this nurse…God forgive me, I married her to get at Ty, because Ty was after her, and because she was nice, and I was so dang miserable after you left and just wanted someone to come home to. It was a huge mistake, a terrible mistake, and in the end she ran off with Ty and…and they were both killed. A car accident. Went off the road on the ice when he'd been drinking." He glanced across at her pinched face. "But I'd told her I wanted to visit San Francisco—she wanted to sit on a beach or some such, and I said no—"

Cassie snorted. A giggle.

"What?"

"I'm…I'm sorry. I didn't mean to—"

"Well, what?"

"Well." She moved beside him and looked him in the eye. "Come on, Coop. The thought of you sitting on a beach is pretty damn funny."

He sat motionless, unable to think straight. "Well, if you understand that about me, why…?" He pivoted toward her, so close he could just lean in and kiss her, so close he could see the flecks in her eyes. "You've cut your hair." His hand went up and slid down the soft satin of it before he pulled back.

"It'll grow. It was just an idea. I was going to look like Twiggy and then realized I'm a mother now and maybe looking like Twiggy doesn't fit the part."

He just stared at her. There she was. After all this time. Cassie. Right there.

"So you were saying about San Francisco?"

"So I went off the first day. She—Barbara—was napping, and I went around Haight-Ashbury hoping to bump into you, find you, asking around. Finally someone sent me to this commune and there, of all the damn people, was Dave."

"Oh, shit. Dave."

"Yeah. Dave. He told me you'd been there and gone off with some man. When was Jacky born, then?"

"Jacky was born by then. The people in the commune were really good about her at first, but then they got fed up with the night crying and having to babysit when I worked. And then I lost my job—"

"Now I remember. You worked in a café or something, didn't you? Someone directed me there, and I asked about you, and the man in the café was the one who sent me on to the commune." He sat for a moment, thinking it through, then reached in his rear jeans pocket and pulled out the folded label to hand to her.

"Where the hell did you get this?"

"Some street market café Barb and I stopped at. I

tried to find out where they got it, but the guy wasn't interested in telling me, I guess." He rested his head in his hand, got a hold on his emotions, and gazed at her.

She handed it back. "I was in Bolinas by then."

"Bolinas? Where's that?"

"Up the coast a bit. Tiny town, full of dropouts and poets and artists and such. I got work living with this wonderful gay couple, and we really hit it off. They loved Jacky and were great to us. And I did gardening and the pies on the side. Then one of them died—it was awful, just awful—and the other left, so I came home."

"You never married?"

"Mommy!"

He watched as she got up and walked up to the screen, talked softly to Jacky, said she'd be in, in a minute.

"Sorry." She sat back down next to him.

"What for?"

She looked at him, her smile as he had remembered it, dreamed about it, longed for it. "The interruption. Everything. Everything, I guess. And no, I never married. Though I was asked." She hesitated. "You were never far from my thoughts, Coop. You should know that."

He sat, his hands hanging in his lap. "It's not your fault. Jeez. I guess I was some sort of bastard, huh? I just always thought 'I love you' were empty words and showing love was far more important. I *thought* I had showed you I loved you. My father used to tell me, 'Oh, sure, I love your mother,' but he never did a damn thing for her. I didn't want to be that way. I just… Damn, Cassie, it was love at first sight. I never felt that way about anyone, but I guess…" He was lost in his own thoughts for a moment. "Why did you come, then? Why did you stop in Jackson?"

"I was so close. Dropped this guy, Gary, in Nebraska, after his partner died and he sold the house, and somehow it just seemed like it was time, for once and for all, to lay the ghosts to sleep. All those years, every time I looked at Jacky I saw you there, a constant reminder, and I thought…I thought…well, you should know. We have this beautiful daughter. Something wonderful came out of those nine months. You had a right to know." She held out the ring for him to take.

He was crying again, blew his nose, looked at the ring in her hand. "You keep it, will you?"

She held it in the flat of her palm, met his gaze, and then slipped the ring on her left ring finger. "Fits perfectly. How did you know?"

He chortled. "I didn't. They made it with that space so it could be taken in or expanded without ruining the inscription. Do you like it?"

"I love it." She studied him, all those feelings she had suffocated for so long, pocketed in a corner of her heart, now overflowing, rising to the surface, the flotsam and jetsam of her life. "And I—"

"MOMMY!"

Cassie got up and strolled to the screen door, bent, and picked up their daughter. "You little minx. Can't you wait a minute for Mama?"

"It was more than a minute."

Cassie set her down beside him.

He studied his daughter, his heart brimming. He could see himself in her, but he could see Cassie as well, a perfect combination of them both, flawless in every way. Her little curls of pigtail jiggled as she tilted her head to look right back at him.

"Who's that?" Jacky's little pointer finger stretched out as she leaned back into her mother's arms.

"That's Coop, sweetheart. That's your daddy."

A word about the author…

A native New Yorker who has spent most of her life living in the U.K., Andrea Downing currently divides her time between the canyons of city streets and the wide-open spaces of Wyoming.

Her background in publishing and English Language teaching has transferred into fiction writing, and her love of horses, ranches, rodeo, and just about anything else western, is reflected in her award-winning historical and contemporary western romances. She has finaled twice for the RONE Awards, and won both the Golden Quill for Best Novella and the Maple Leaf Award for Favorite Hero, as well as several other honors.

You can find out more about her books at:

http://andreadowning.com

Thank you for purchasing
this publication of The Wild Rose Press, Inc.

For questions or more information
contact us at
info@thewildrosepress.com.

The Wild Rose Press, Inc.
www.thewildrosepress.com